JURASSIC PARK

VOLUME 3

DON'T MOVE!

ADAPTED BY
WALTER SIMONSON,
GIL KANE AND GEORGE PEREZ

Spotlight

visit us at www.abdopublishing.com

Reinforced library bound editions published in 2014 by Spotlight, a division of the ABDO Group, PO Box 398166, Minneapolis, Minnesota 55439. Published by agreement with IDW Publishing. www.idwpublishing.com

Printed in the United States of America, North Mankato, Minnesota.
052013
092013
♻ This book contains at least 10% recycled materials.

Library of Congress Cataloging-in-Publication Data

Simonson, Walter.
 Jurassic Park / adapted by Walter Simonson, Gil Kane, and George Perez.
    pages cm
  ISBN 978-1-61479-183-6 (vol. 1: Danger) -- ISBN 978-1-61479-184-3 (vol. 2: The miracle of cloning) -- ISBN 978-1-61479-185-0 (vol. 3: Don't move!) -- ISBN 978-1-61479-186-7 (vol. 4: Leaving Jurassic Park)
 1. Graphic novels. I. Kane, Gil. II. Perez, George, 1954- III. Title.
  PZ7.7.S5465Jur 2013
  741.5'973--dc23
                    2013011263

All Spotlight books are reinforced library binding and manufactured in the United States of America.

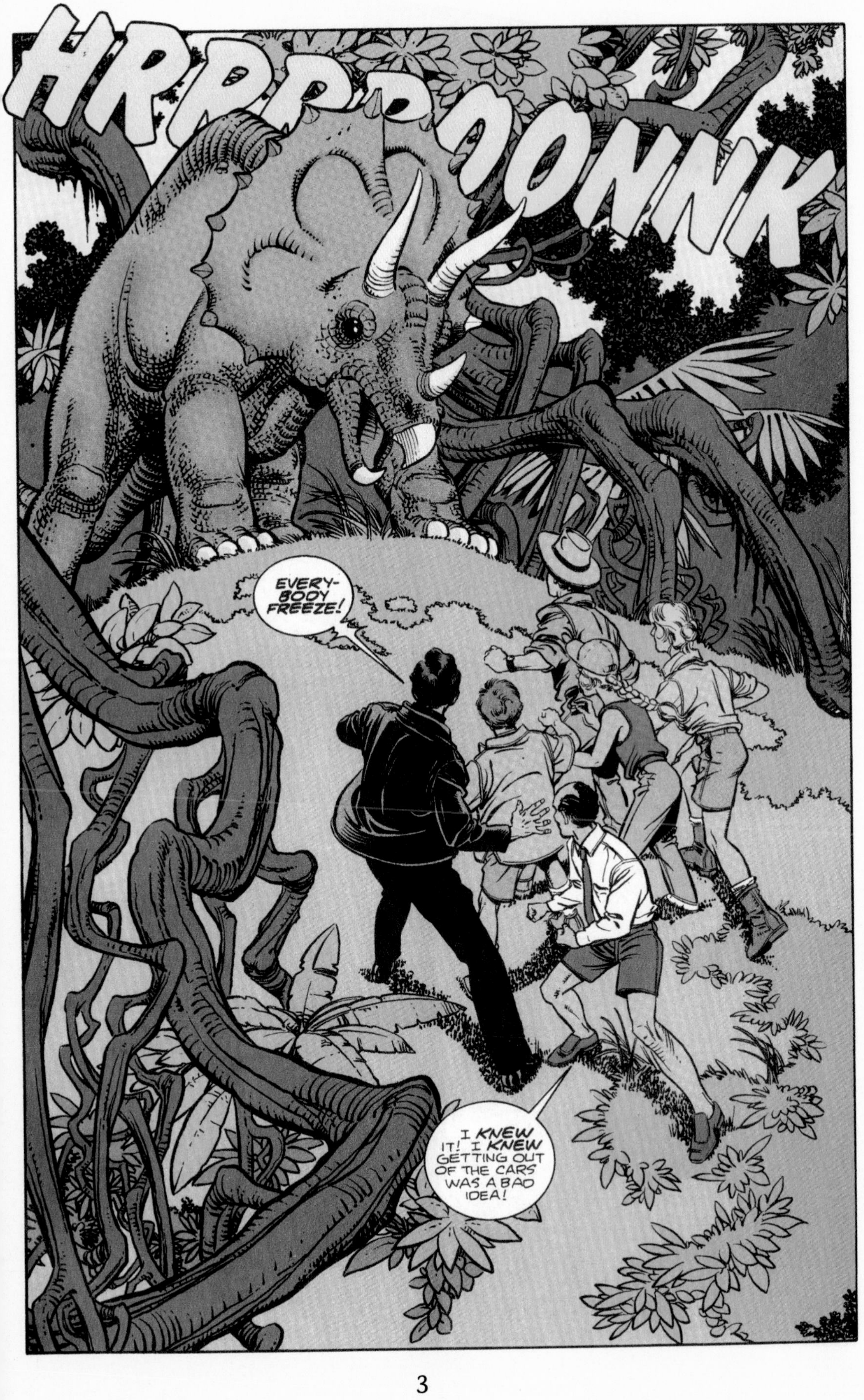

HRRRROONNK
EVERY-BODY FREEZE!
I KNEW IT! I KNEW GETTING OUT OF THE CARS WAS A BAD IDEA!

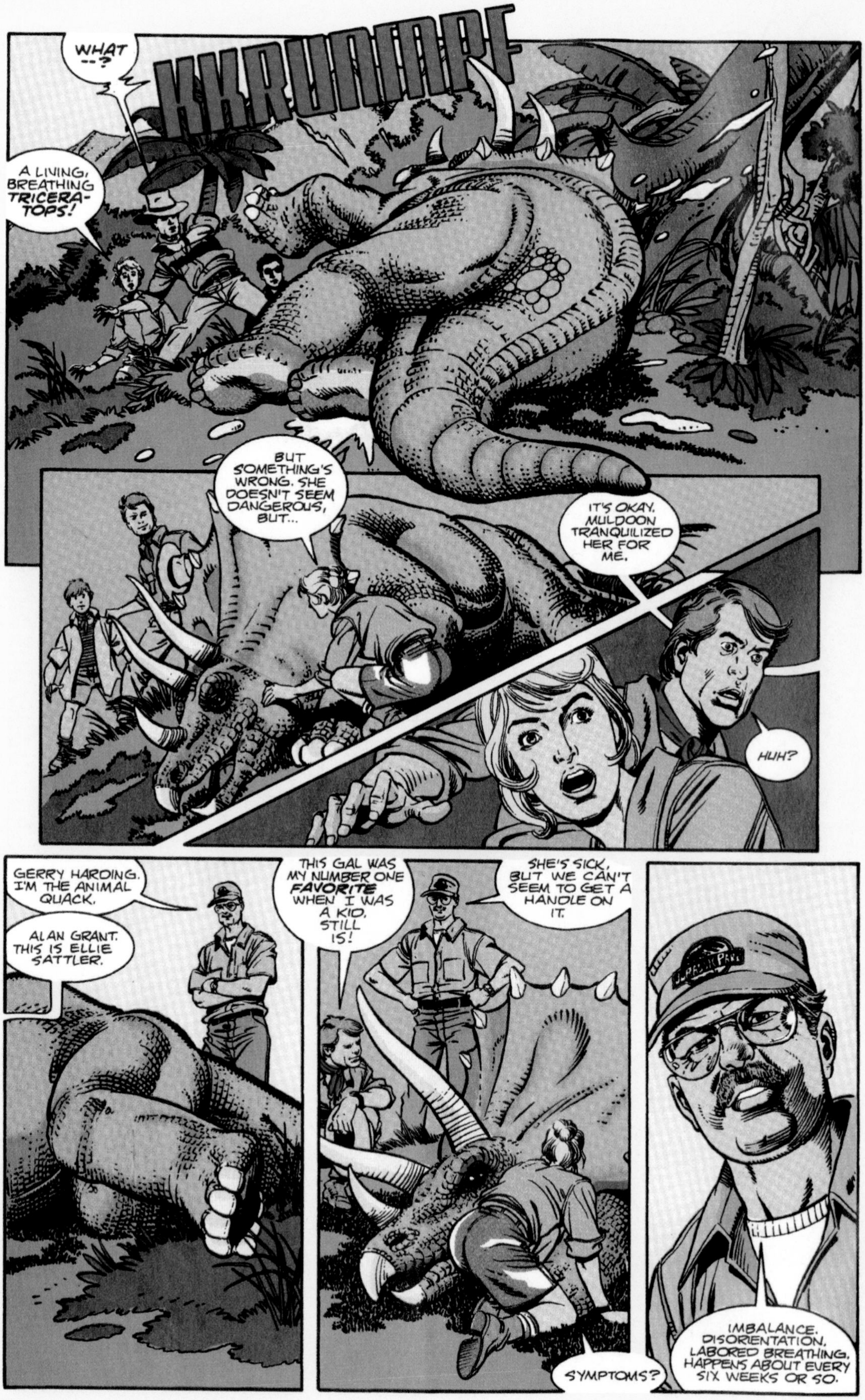
WHAT --?
KKRUNMPF
A LIVING, BREATHING TRICERA-TOPS!
BUT SOMETHING'S WRONG. SHE DOESN'T SEEM DANGEROUS, BUT...
IT'S OKAY. MULDOON TRANQUILIZED HER FOR ME.
HUH?
GERRY HARDING. I'M THE ANIMAL QUACK.
ALAN GRANT. THIS IS ELLIE SATTLER.
THIS GAL WAS MY NUMBER ONE FAVORITE WHEN I WAS A KID. STILL IS!
SHE'S SICK, BUT WE CAN'T SEEM TO GET A HANDLE ON IT.
SYMPTOMS?
IMBALANCE. DISORIENTATION. LABORED BREATHING. HAPPENS ABOUT EVERY SIX WEEKS OR SO.

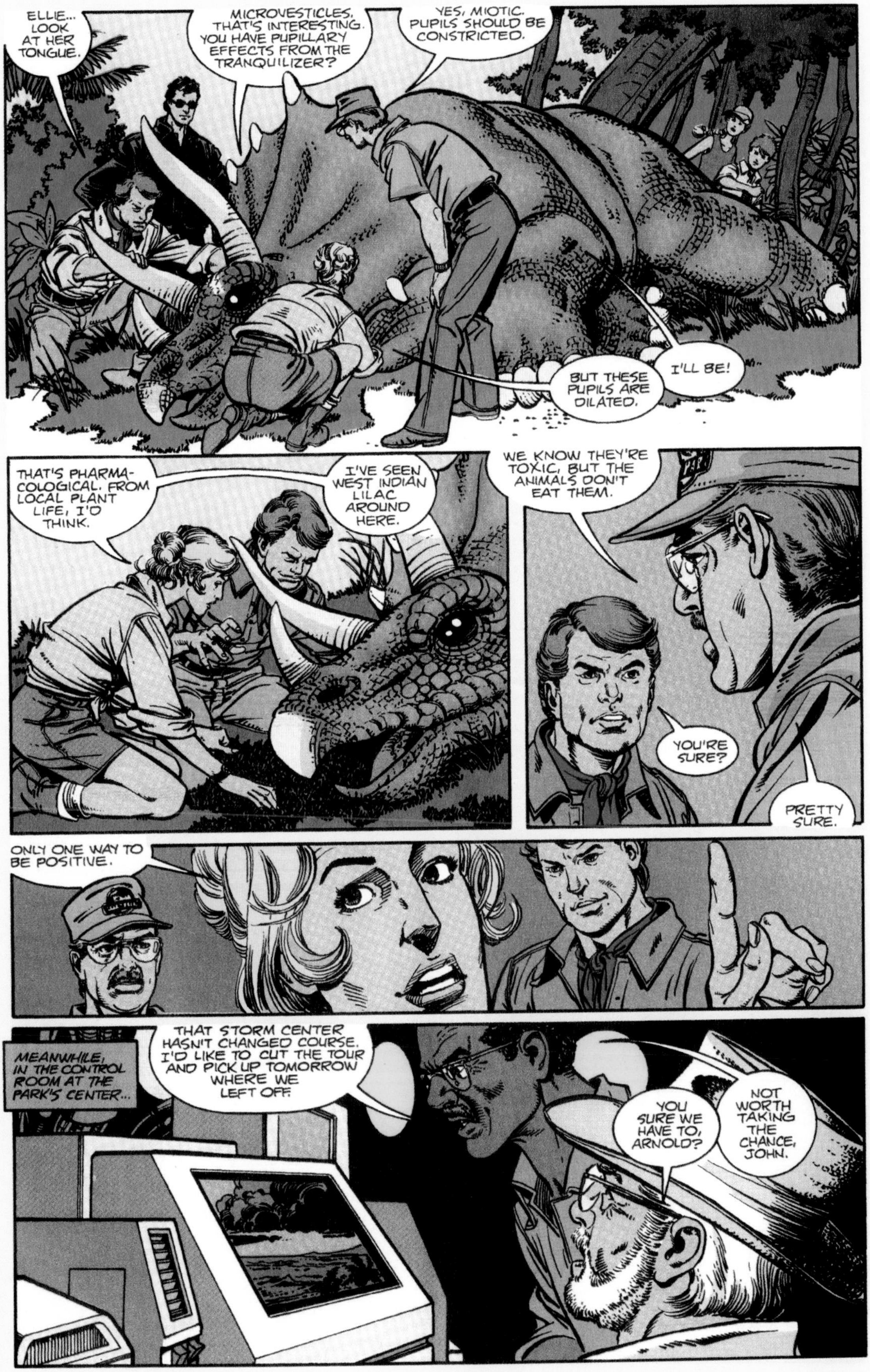
ELLIE... LOOK AT HER TONGUE.
MICROVESTICLES. THAT'S INTERESTING. YOU HAVE PUPILLARY EFFECTS FROM THE TRANQUILIZER?
YES, MIOTIC. PUPILS SHOULD BE CONSTRICTED.
BUT THESE PUPILS ARE DILATED.
I'LL BE!
THAT'S PHARMA-COLOGICAL. FROM LOCAL PLANT LIFE, I'D THINK.
I'VE SEEN WEST INDIAN LILAC AROUND HERE.
WE KNOW THEY'RE TOXIC, BUT THE ANIMALS DON'T EAT THEM.
YOU'RE SURE?
PRETTY SURE.
ONLY ONE WAY TO BE POSITIVE.
MEANWHILE, IN THE CONTROL ROOM AT THE PARK'S CENTER...
THAT STORM CENTER HASN'T CHANGED COURSE. I'D LIKE TO CUT THE TOUR AND PICK UP TOMORROW WHERE WE LEFT OFF.
YOU SURE WE HAVE TO, ARNOLD?
NOT WORTH TAKING THE CHANCE, JOHN.

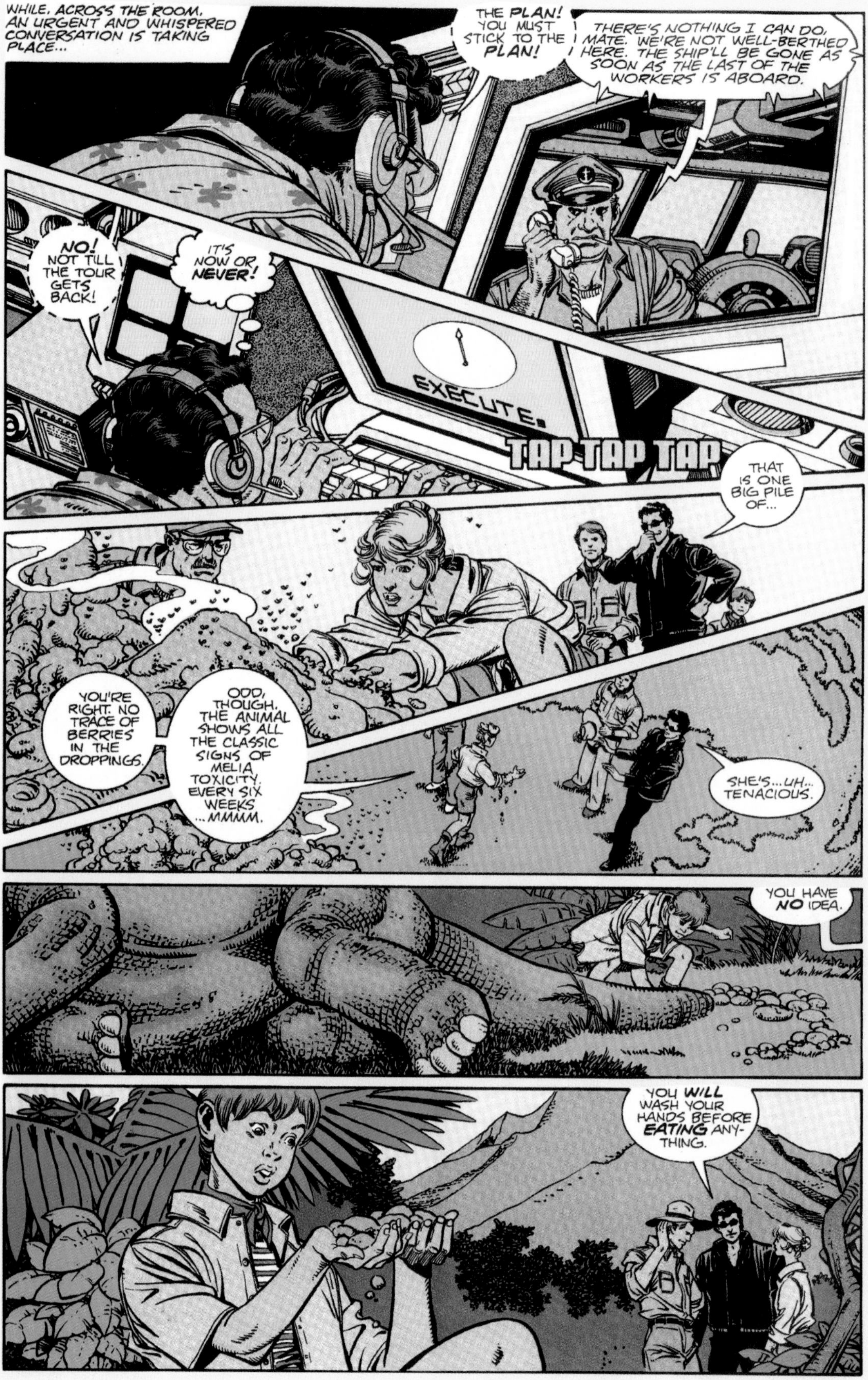
WHILE, ACROSS THE ROOM, AN URGENT AND WHISPERED CONVERSATION IS TAKING PLACE...
THE PLAN! YOU MUST STICK TO THE PLAN!
THERE'S NOTHING I CAN DO, MATE. WE'RE NOT WELL-BERTHED HERE. THE SHIP'LL BE GONE AS SOON AS THE LAST OF THE WORKERS IS ABOARD.
NO! NOT TILL THE TOUR GETS BACK!
IT'S NOW OR NEVER!
EXECUTE.
TAP TAP TAP
THAT IS ONE BIG PILE OF...
YOU'RE RIGHT. NO TRACE OF BERRIES IN THE DROPPINGS.
ODD, THOUGH. THE ANIMAL SHOWS ALL THE CLASSIC SIGNS OF MELIA TOXICITY. EVERY SIX WEEKS ...MMMM.
SHE'S...UH... TENACIOUS.
YOU HAVE NO IDEA.
YOU WILL WASH YOUR HANDS BEFORE EATING ANY-THING.

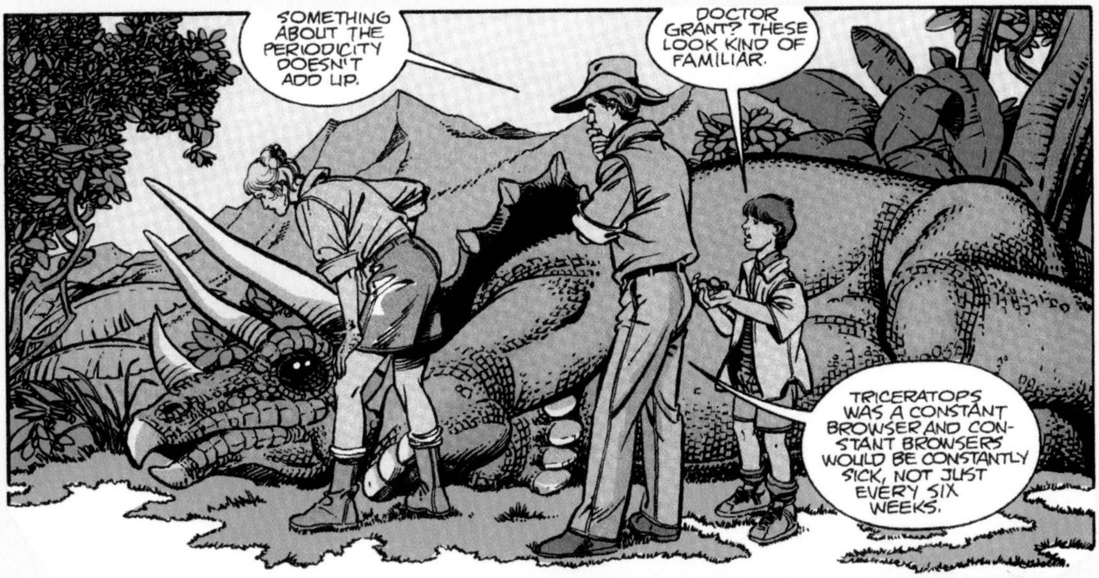
SOMETHING ABOUT THE PERIODICITY DOESN'T ADD UP.
DOCTOR GRANT? THESE LOOK KIND OF FAMILIAR.
TRICERATOPS WAS A CONSTANT BROWSER AND CONSTANT BROWSERS WOULD BE CONSTANTLY SICK, NOT JUST EVERY SIX WEEKS.

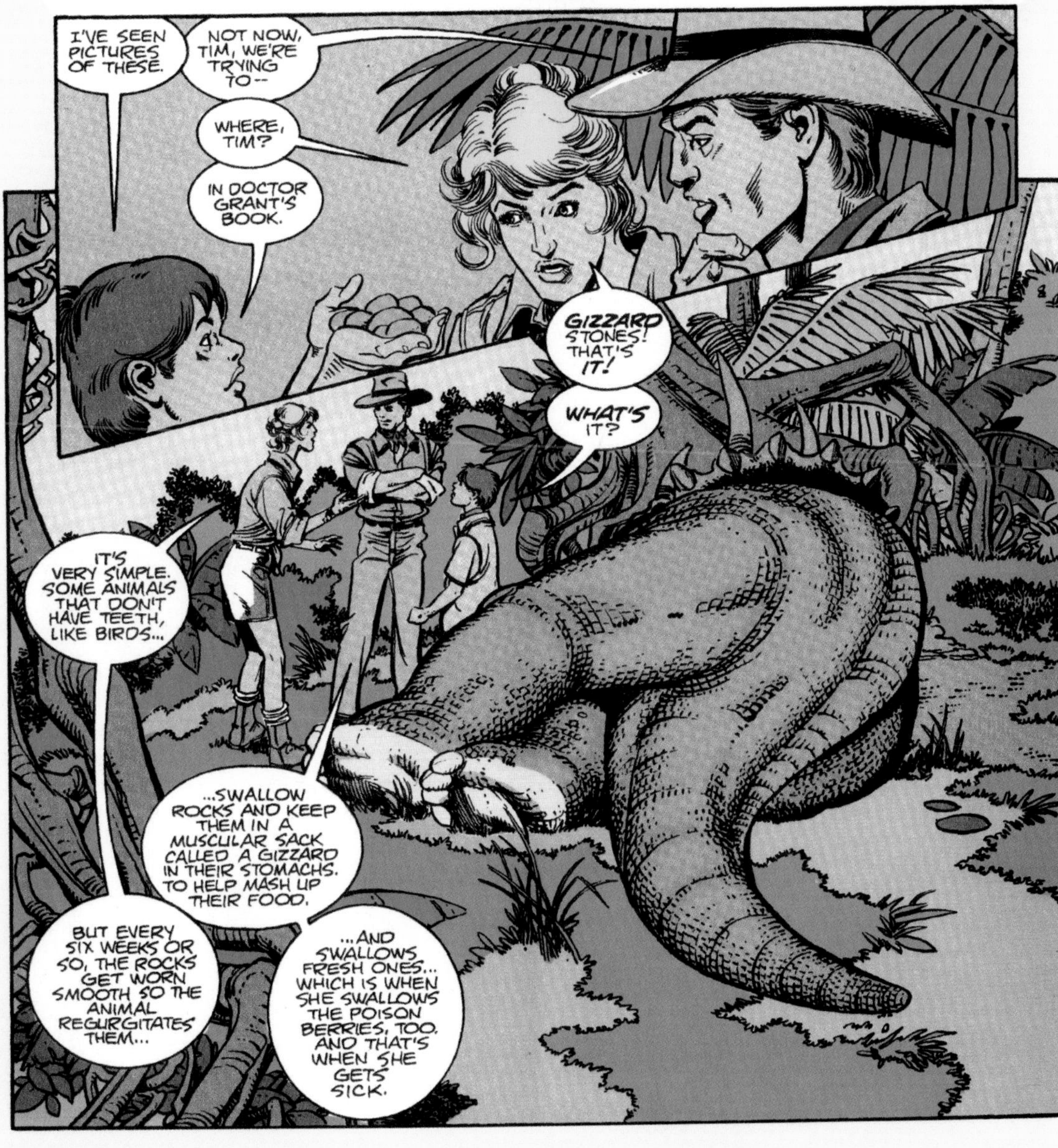
I'VE SEEN PICTURES OF THESE.
NOT NOW, TIM, WE'RE TRYING TO--
WHERE, TIM?
IN DOCTOR GRANT'S BOOK.
GIZZARD STONES! THAT'S IT!
WHAT'S IT?
IT'S VERY SIMPLE. SOME ANIMALS THAT DON'T HAVE TEETH, LIKE BIRDS...
...SWALLOW ROCKS AND KEEP THEM IN A MUSCULAR SACK CALLED A GIZZARD IN THEIR STOMACHS. TO HELP MASH UP THEIR FOOD.
BUT EVERY SIX WEEKS OR SO, THE ROCKS GET WORN SMOOTH SO THE ANIMAL REGURGITATES THEM...
...AND SWALLOWS FRESH ONES... WHICH IS WHEN SHE SWALLOWS THE POISON BERRIES, TOO. AND THAT'S WHEN SHE GETS SICK.

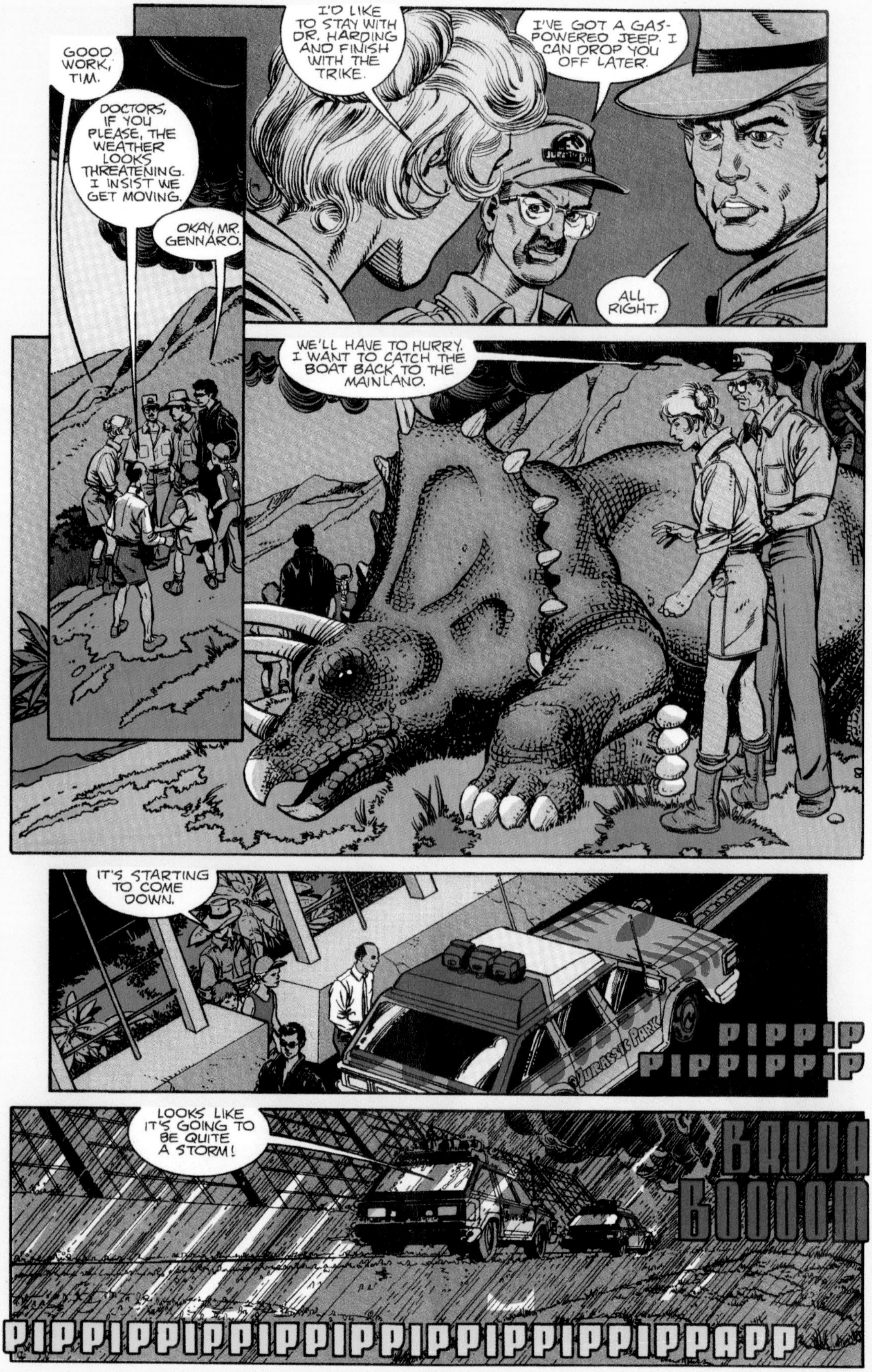
GOOD WORK, TIM.
I'D LIKE TO STAY WITH DR. HARDING AND FINISH WITH THE TRIKE.
I'VE GOT A GAS-POWERED JEEP. I CAN DROP YOU OFF LATER.
DOCTORS, IF YOU PLEASE, THE WEATHER LOOKS THREATENING. I INSIST WE GET MOVING.
OKAY, MR. GENNARO.
ALL RIGHT.
WE'LL HAVE TO HURRY. I WANT TO CATCH THE BOAT BACK TO THE MAINLAND.
IT'S STARTING TO COME DOWN.
PIPPIP
PIPPIPPIP
LOOKS LIKE IT'S GOING TO BE QUITE A STORM!
BADDA
BOOOOM
PIPPIPPIPPIPPIPPIPPIPPIPPIPPIPPIPPAPP

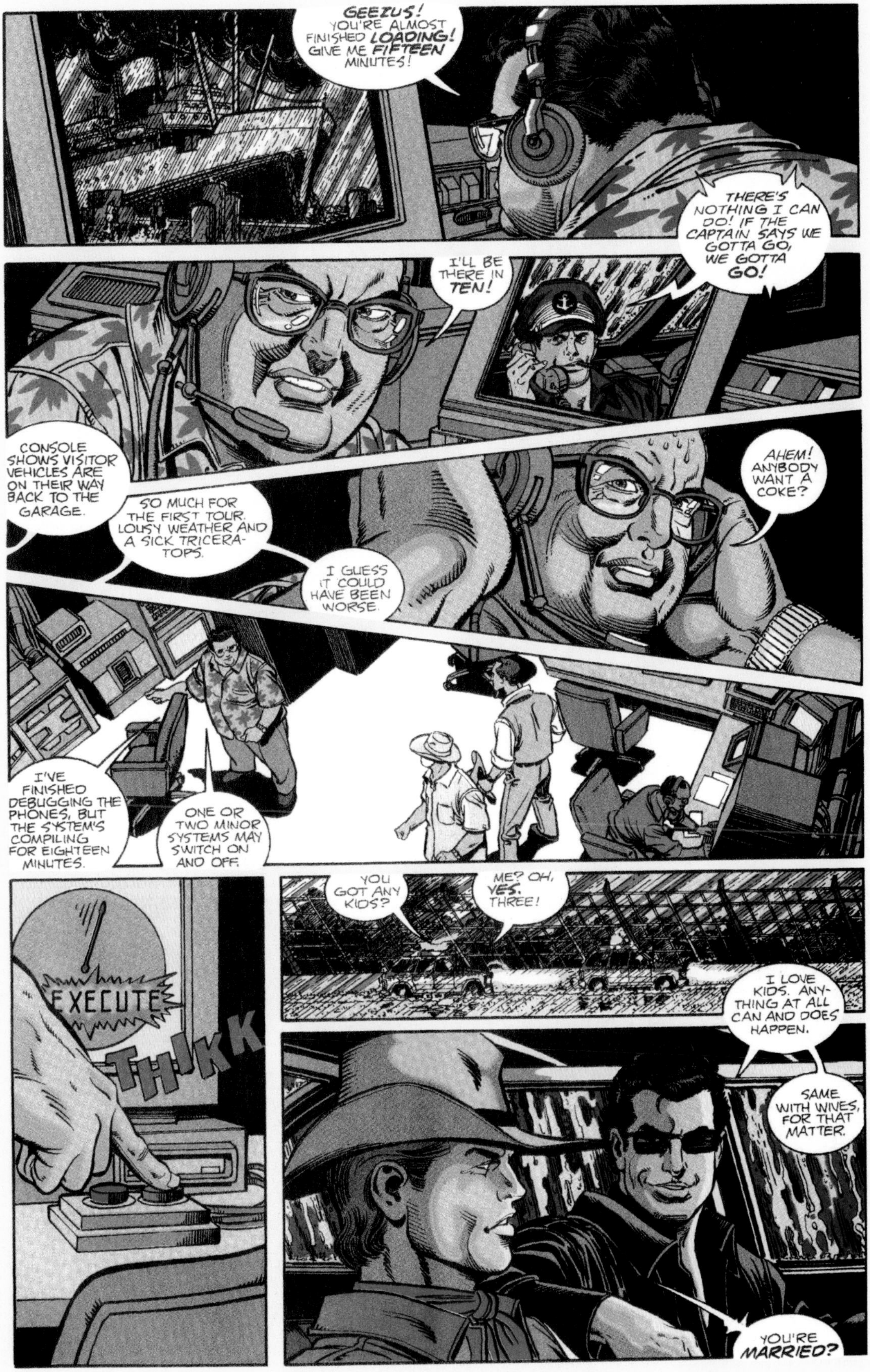
GEEZUS! YOU'RE ALMOST FINISHED LOADING! GIVE ME FIFTEEN MINUTES!
THERE'S NOTHING I CAN DO! IF THE CAPTAIN SAYS WE GOTTA GO, WE GOTTA GO!
I'LL BE THERE IN TEN!
CONSOLE SHOWS VISITOR VEHICLES ARE ON THEIR WAY BACK TO THE GARAGE.
SO MUCH FOR THE FIRST TOUR. LOUSY WEATHER AND A SICK TRICERATOPS.
I GUESS IT COULD HAVE BEEN WORSE.
AHEM! ANYBODY WANT A COKE?
I'VE FINISHED DEBUGGING THE PHONES, BUT THE SYSTEM'S COMPILING FOR EIGHTEEN MINUTES.
ONE OR TWO MINOR SYSTEMS MAY SWITCH ON AND OFF.
EXECUTE
THIKK
YOU GOT ANY KIDS?
ME? OH, YES. THREE!
I LOVE KIDS. ANYTHING AT ALL CAN AND DOES HAPPEN.
SAME WITH WIVES, FOR THAT MATTER.
YOU'RE MARRIED?

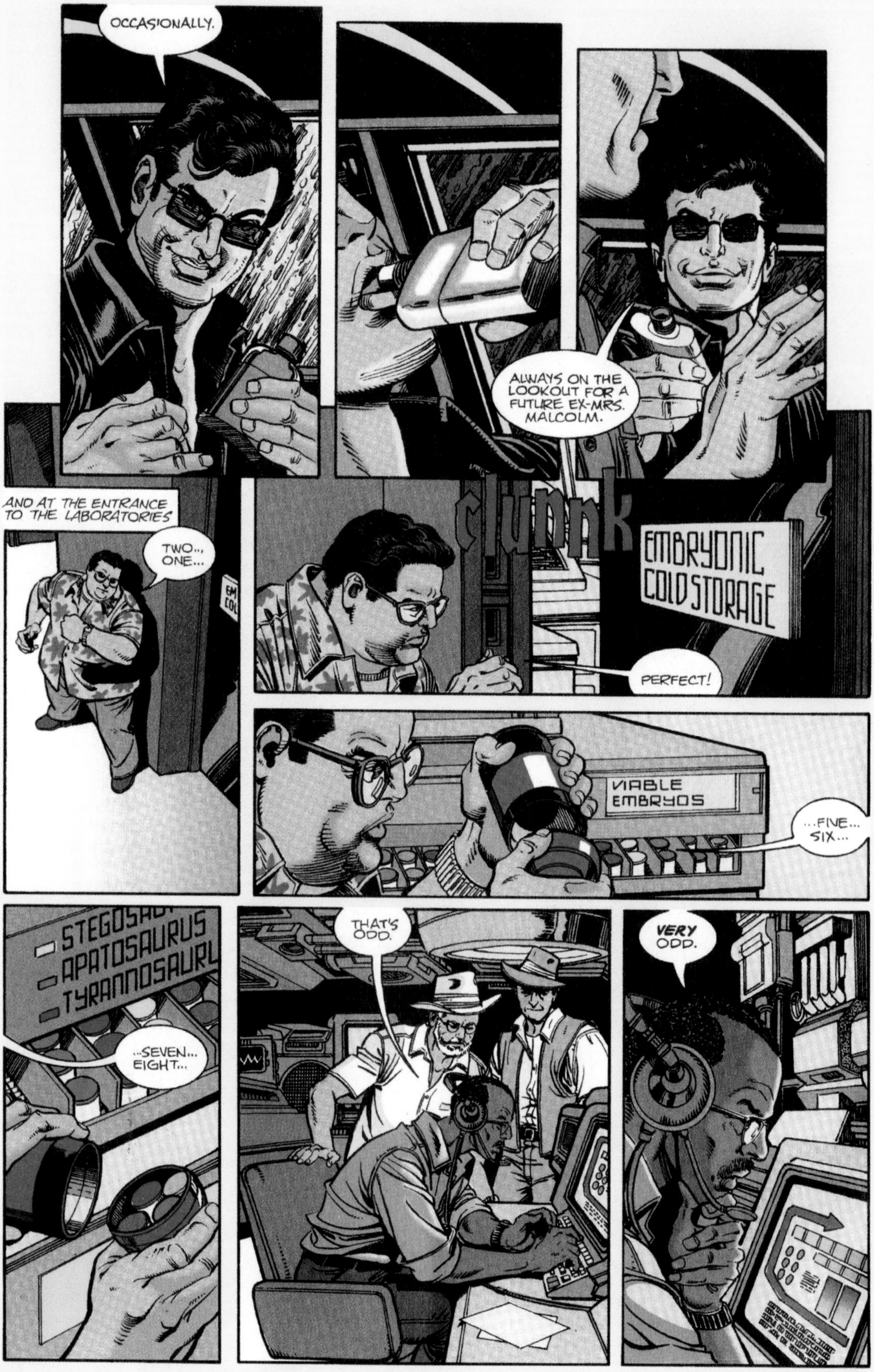
OCCASIONALLY.
ALWAYS ON THE LOOKOUT FOR A FUTURE EX-MRS. MALCOLM.
AND AT THE ENTRANCE TO THE LABORATORIES
TWO..., ONE...
clunnk
EMBRYONIC COLD STORAGE
PERFECT!
VIABLE EMBRYOS
...FIVE... SIX...
STEGOSAU
APATOSAURUS
TYRANNOSAURU
...SEVEN... EIGHT...
THAT'S ODD.
VERY ODD.

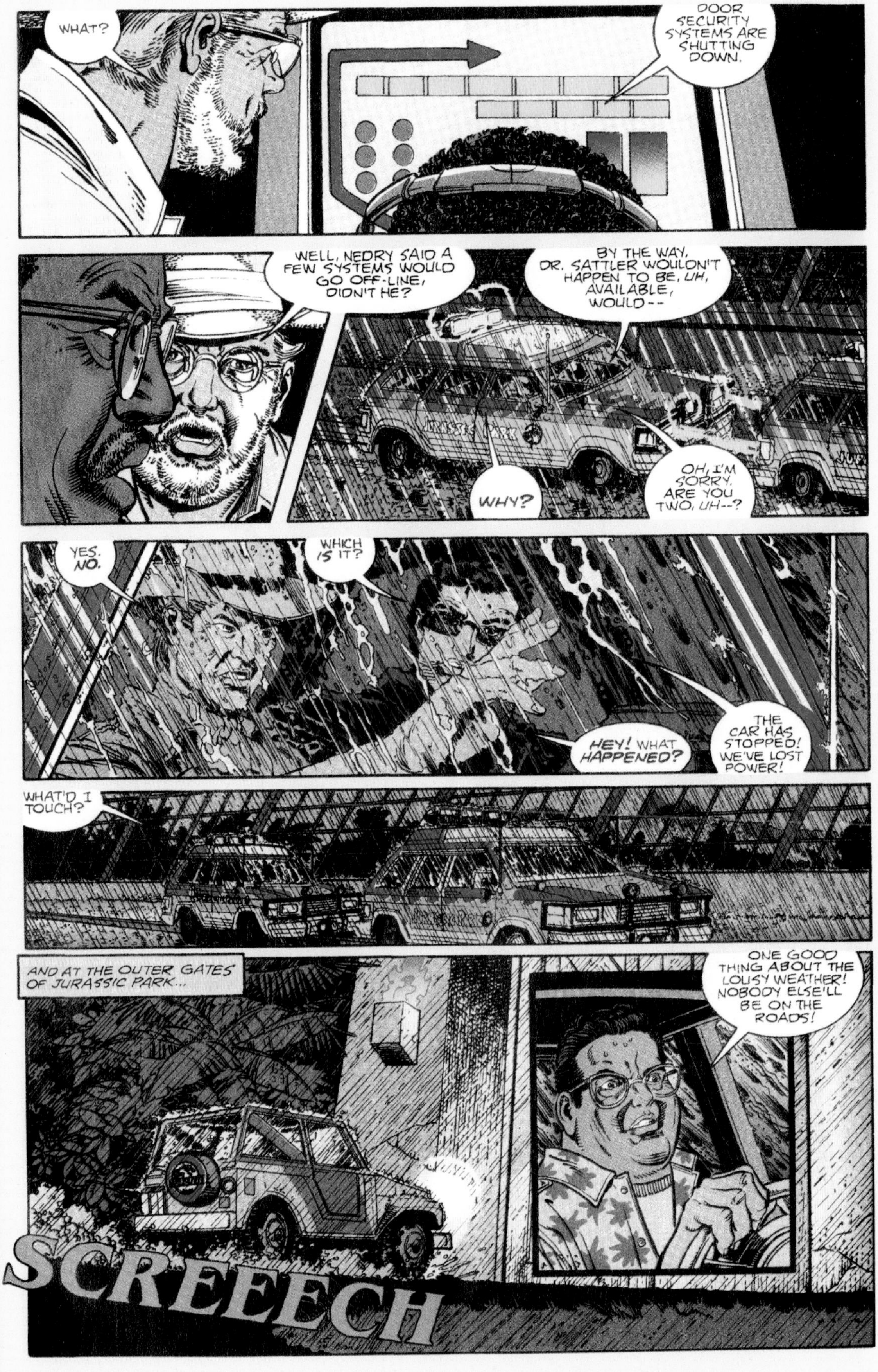
WHAT?
DOOR SECURITY SYSTEMS ARE SHUTTING DOWN.
WELL, NEDRY SAID A FEW SYSTEMS WOULD GO OFF-LINE, DIDN'T HE?
BY THE WAY, DR. SATTLER WOULDN'T HAPPEN TO BE, UH, AVAILABLE, WOULD--
WHY?
OH, I'M SORRY. ARE YOU TWO, UH--?
YES. NO.
WHICH IS IT?
HEY! WHAT HAPPENED?
THE CAR HAS STOPPED! WE'VE LOST POWER!
WHAT'D I TOUCH?
AND AT THE OUTER GATES OF JURASSIC PARK...
ONE GOOD THING ABOUT THE LOUSY WEATHER! NOBODY ELSE'LL BE ON THE ROADS!
SCREEECH

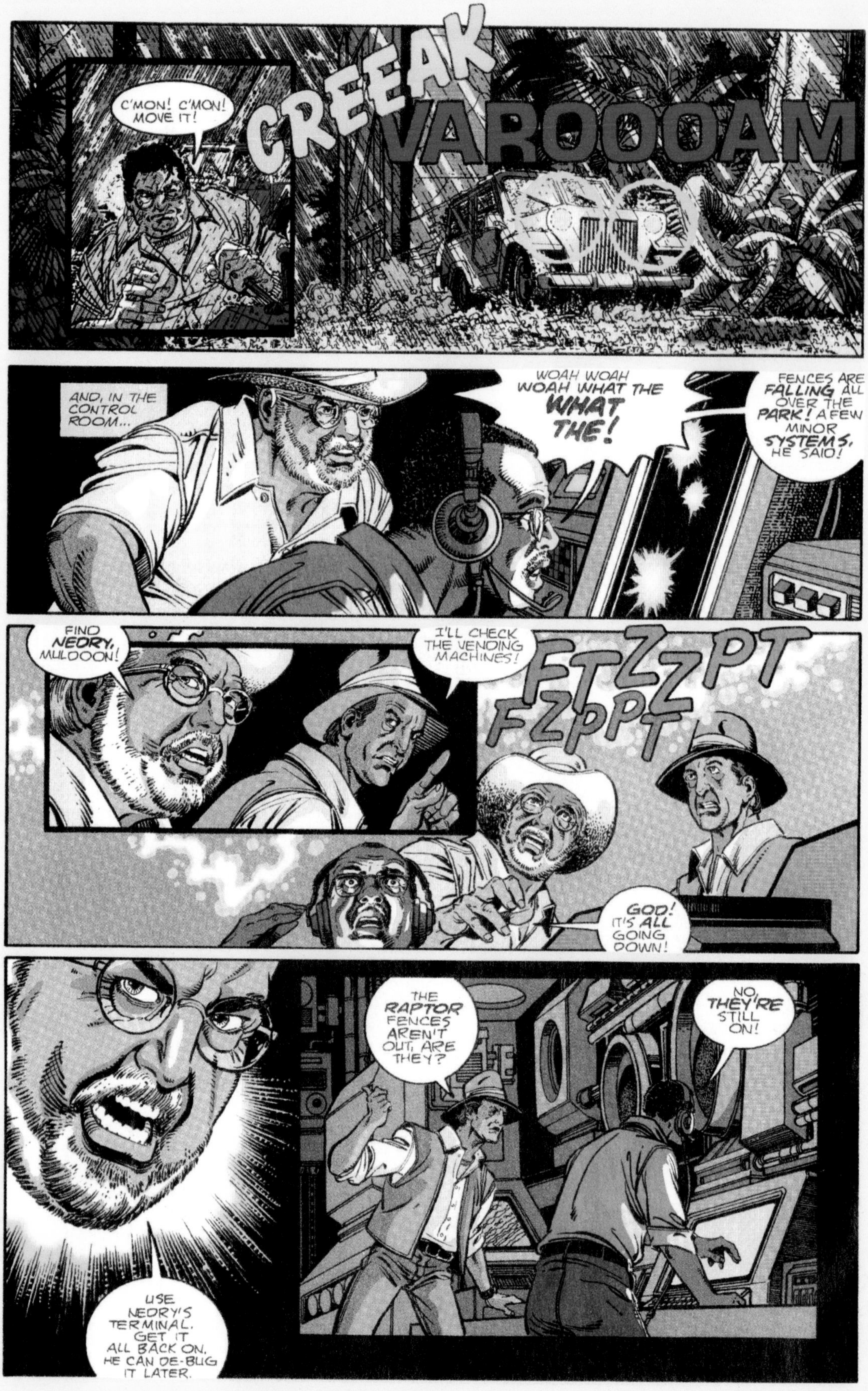

C'MON! C'MON! MOVE IT!
CREEAK
VAROOOAM
AND, IN THE CONTROL ROOM...
WOAH WOAH WOAH WHAT THE WHAT THE!
FENCES ARE FALLING ALL OVER THE PARK! A FEW MINOR SYSTEMS, HE SAID!
FIND NEDRY, MULDOON!
I'LL CHECK THE VENDING MACHINES!
FTZZZPT
FZPPT
GOD! IT'S ALL GOING DOWN!
USE NEDRY'S TERMINAL. GET IT ALL BACK ON. HE CAN DE-BUG IT LATER.
THE RAPTOR FENCES AREN'T OUT, ARE THEY?
NO, THEY'RE STILL ON!

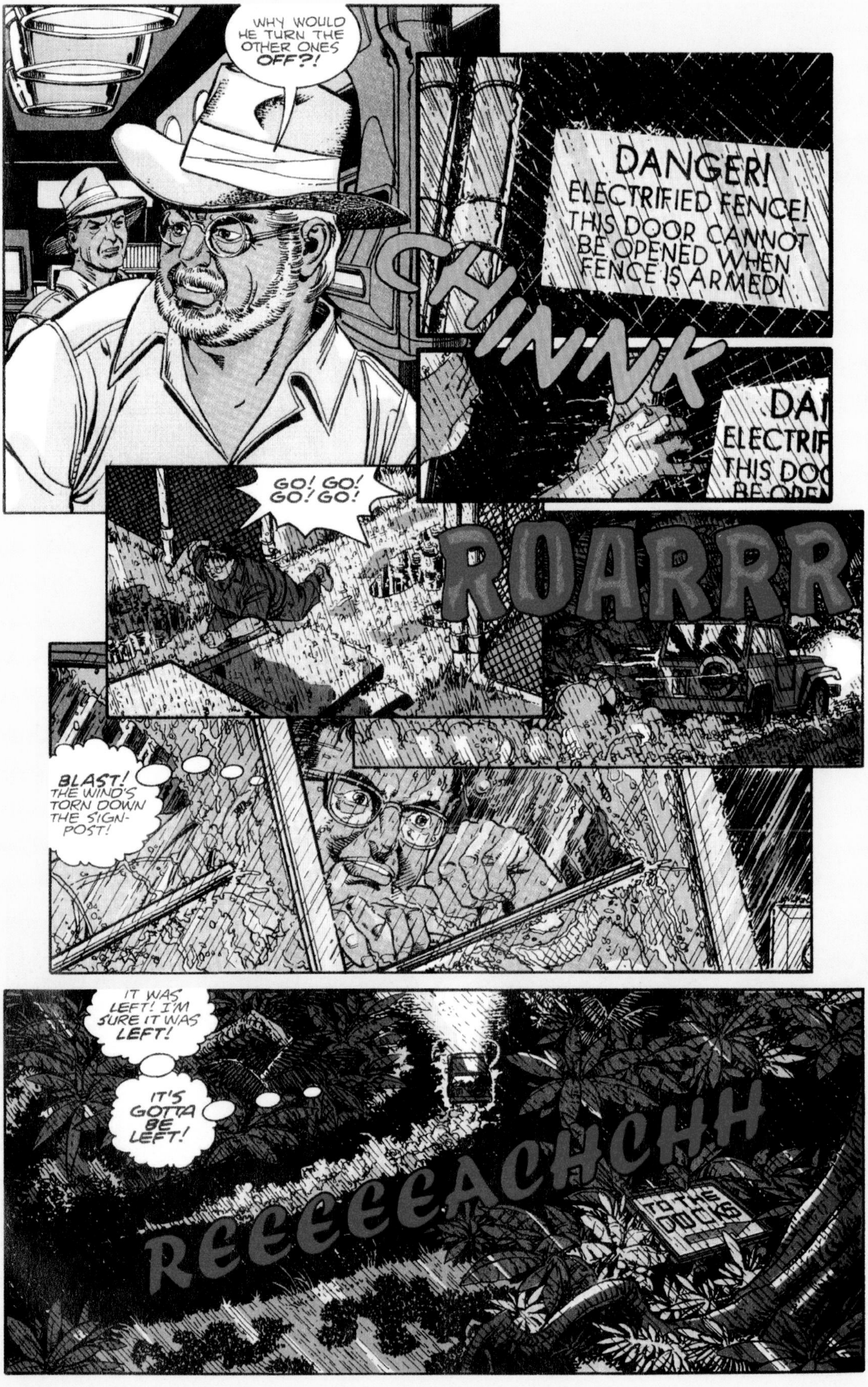
WHY WOULD HE TURN THE OTHER ONES OFF?!
DANGER! ELECTRIFIED FENCE! THIS DOOR CANNOT BE OPENED WHEN FENCE IS ARMED!
CHINNK
GO! GO! GO! GO!
ROARRR
BLAST! THE WIND'S TORN DOWN THE SIGN-POST!
IT WAS LEFT! I'M SURE IT WAS LEFT!
IT'S GOTTA BE LEFT!
REEEEEACHCHH
TO THE DOCKS

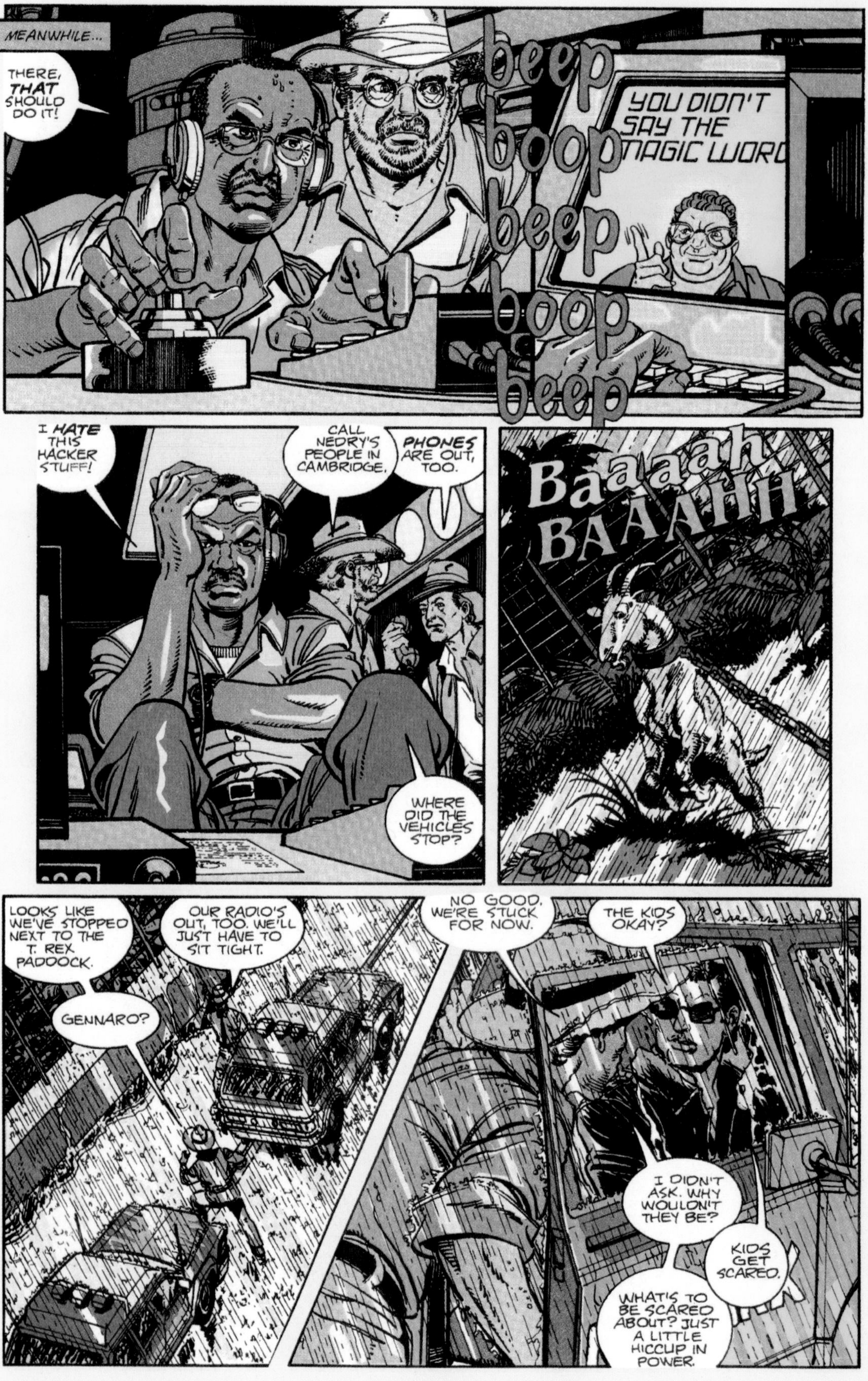
MEANWHILE...
THERE, THAT SHOULD DO IT!
beep boop beep boop beep
YOU DIDN'T SAY THE MAGIC WORD
I HATE THIS HACKER STUFF!
CALL NEDRY'S PEOPLE IN CAMBRIDGE.
PHONES ARE OUT, TOO.
WHERE DID THE VEHICLES STOP?
Baaaaah BAAAHH
LOOKS LIKE WE'VE STOPPED NEXT TO THE T. REX PADDOCK.
GENNARO?
OUR RADIO'S OUT, TOO. WE'LL JUST HAVE TO SIT TIGHT.
NO GOOD. WE'RE STUCK FOR NOW.
THE KIDS OKAY?
I DIDN'T ASK. WHY WOULDN'T THEY BE?
KIDS GET SCARED.
WHAT'S TO BE SCARED ABOUT? JUST A LITTLE HICCUP IN POWER.

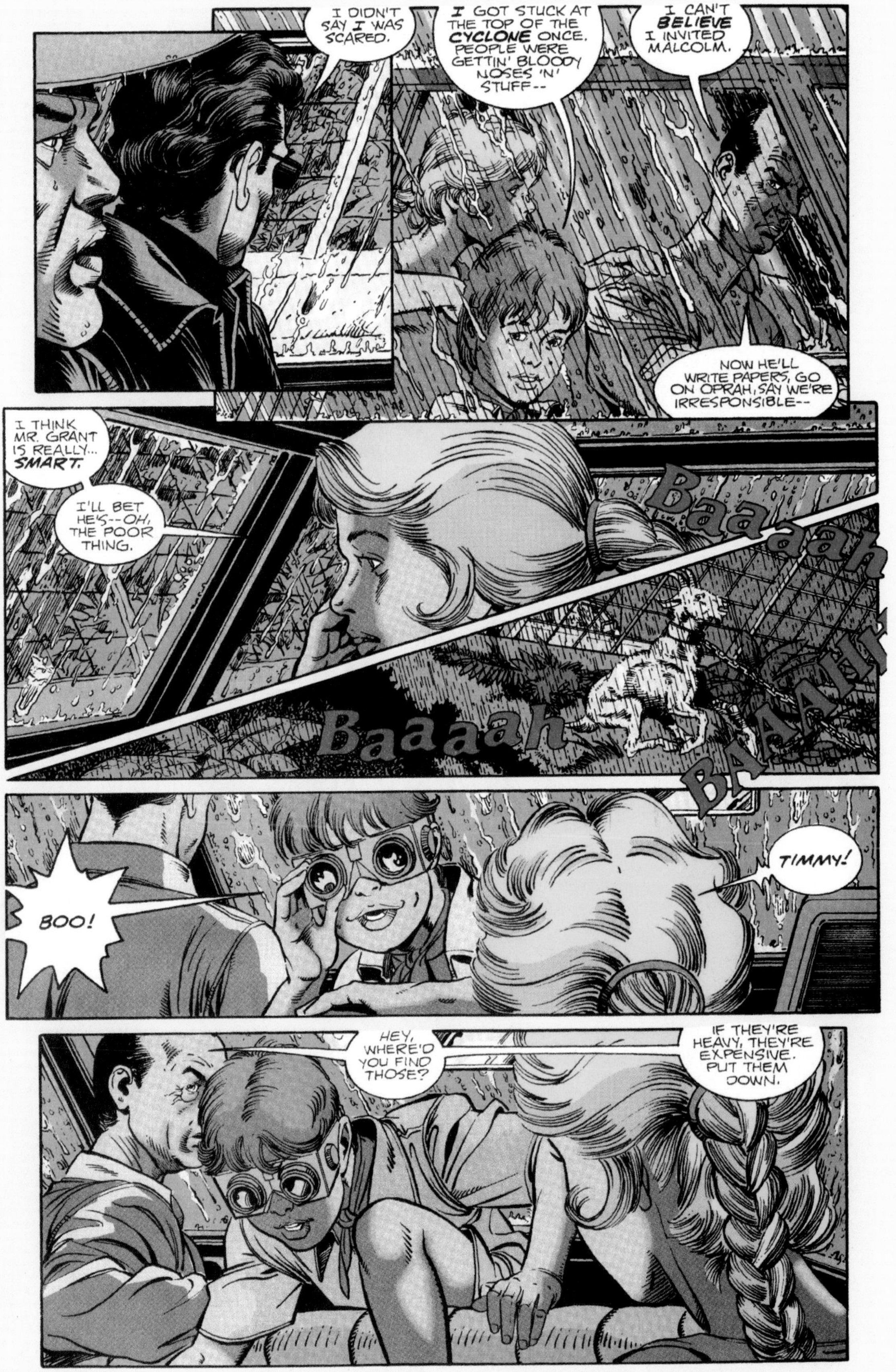
I DIDN'T SAY I WAS SCARED.
I GOT STUCK AT THE TOP OF THE CYCLONE ONCE. PEOPLE WERE GETTIN' BLOODY NOSES 'N' STUFF--
I CAN'T BELIEVE I INVITED MALCOLM.
NOW HE'LL WRITE PAPERS, GO ON OPRAH, SAY WE'RE IRRESPONSIBLE--
I THINK MR. GRANT IS REALLY... SMART.
I'LL BET HE'S--OH, THE POOR THING.
Baaaah
Baaaah
BAAAH
BOO!
TIMMY!
HEY, WHERE'D YOU FIND THOSE?
IF THEY'RE HEAVY, THEY'RE EXPENSIVE. PUT THEM DOWN.

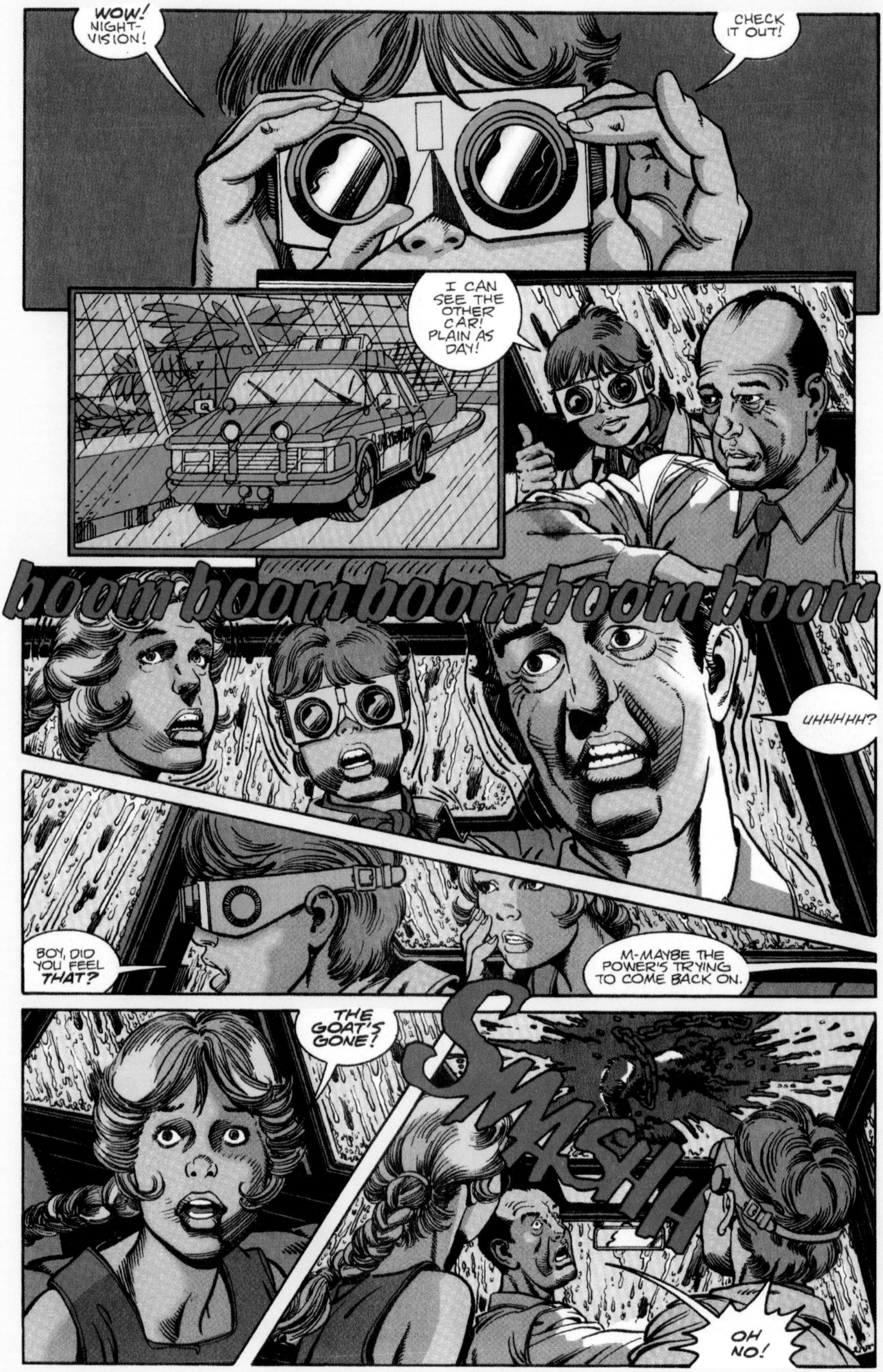

WOW! NIGHT-VISION!
CHECK IT OUT!
I CAN SEE THE OTHER CAR! PLAIN AS DAY!
boom boom boom boom boom
UHHHHH?
BOY, DID YOU FEEL THAT?
M-MAYBE THE POWER'S TRYING TO COME BACK ON.
THE GOAT'S GONE!
SMASHH
OH NO!

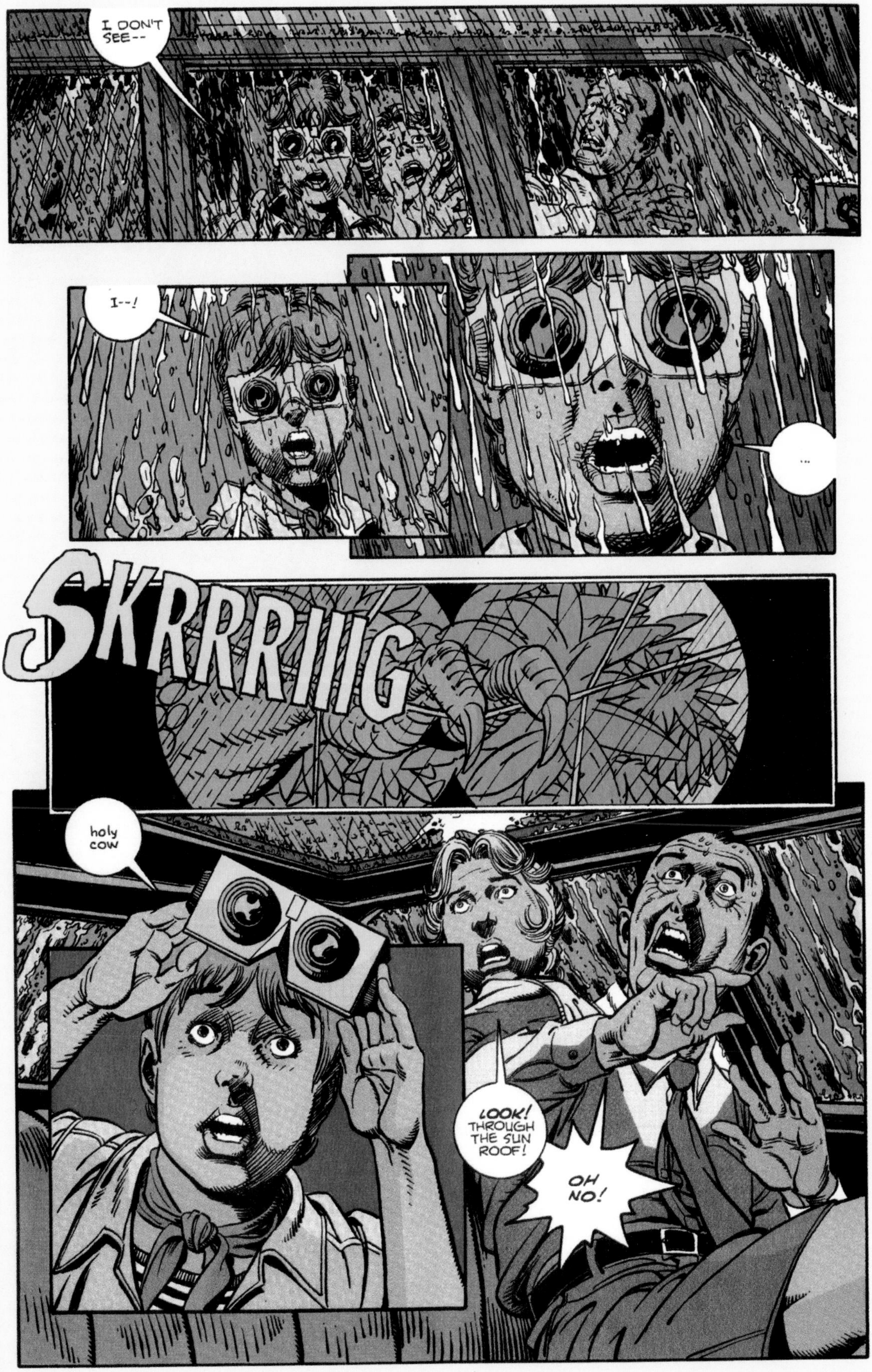

I DON'T SEE--
I--!
...
SKRRRIIIG
holy cow
LOOK! THROUGH THE SUN ROOF!
OH NO!

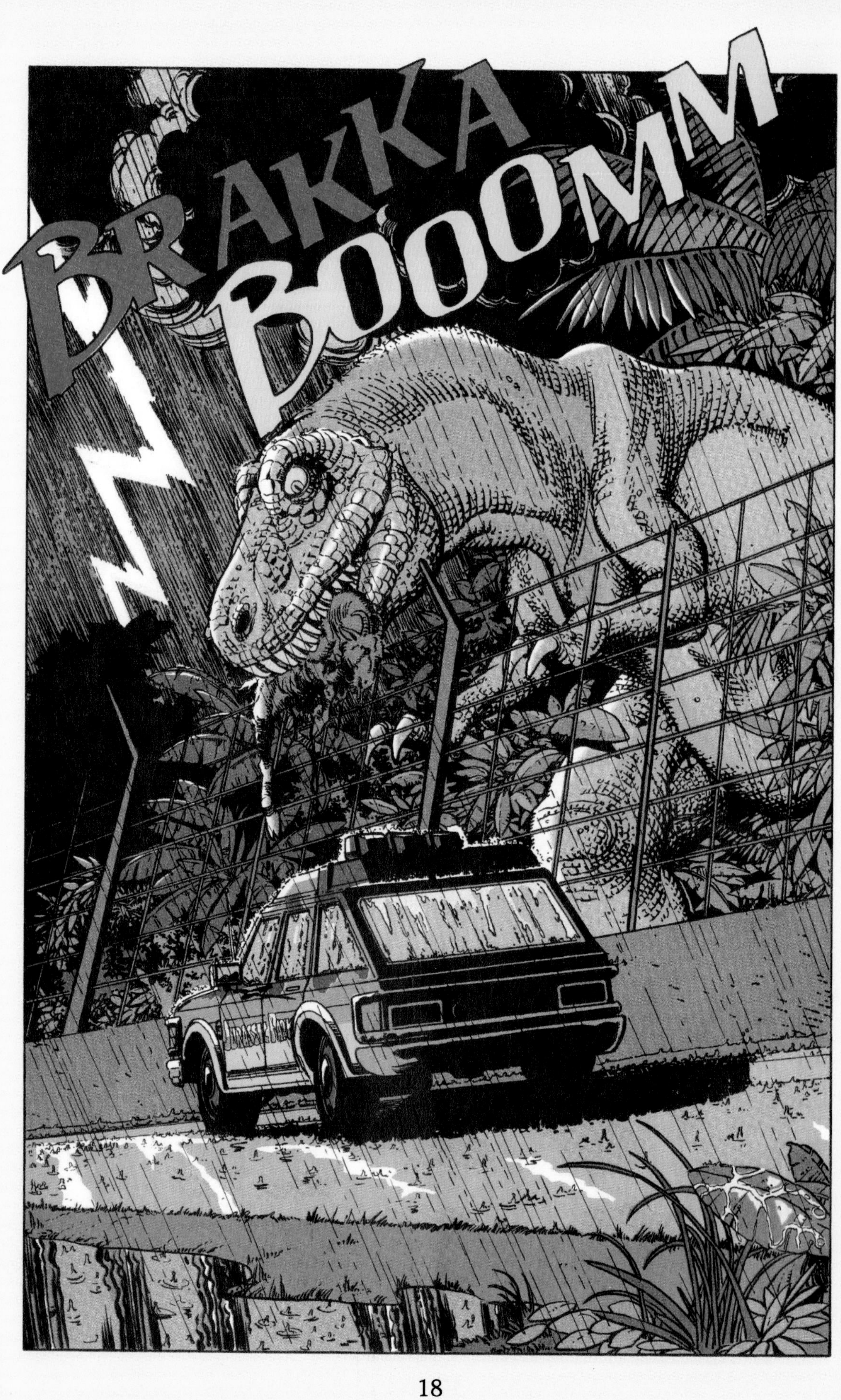
BRAKKA
BOOOMM
JURASSIC PARK

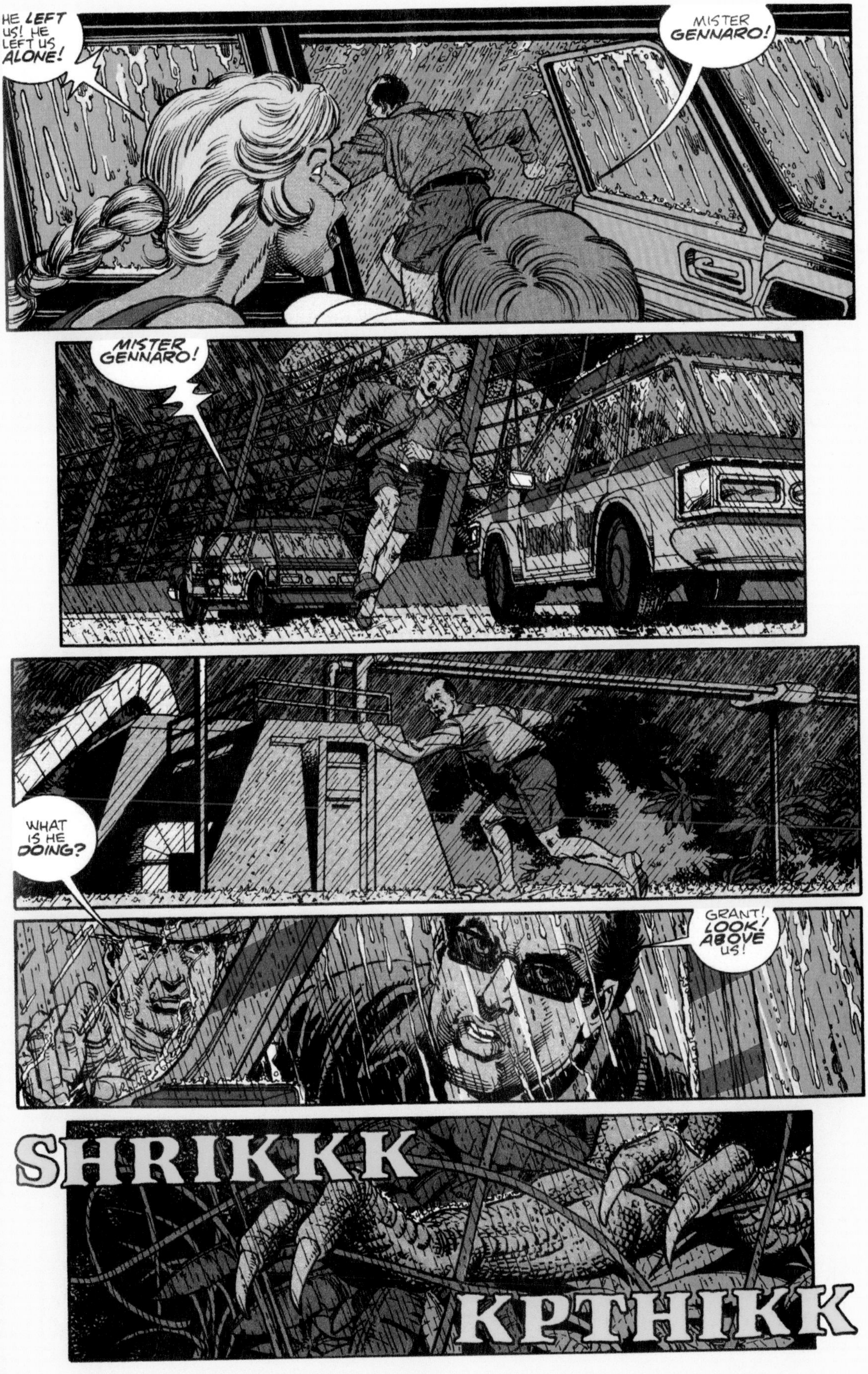

HE *LEFT* US! HE LEFT US *ALONE*!
MISTER *GENNARO!*
MISTER GENNARO!
WHAT IS HE *DOING?*
GRANT! *LOOK! ABOVE* US!
SHRIKKK
KPTHIKK

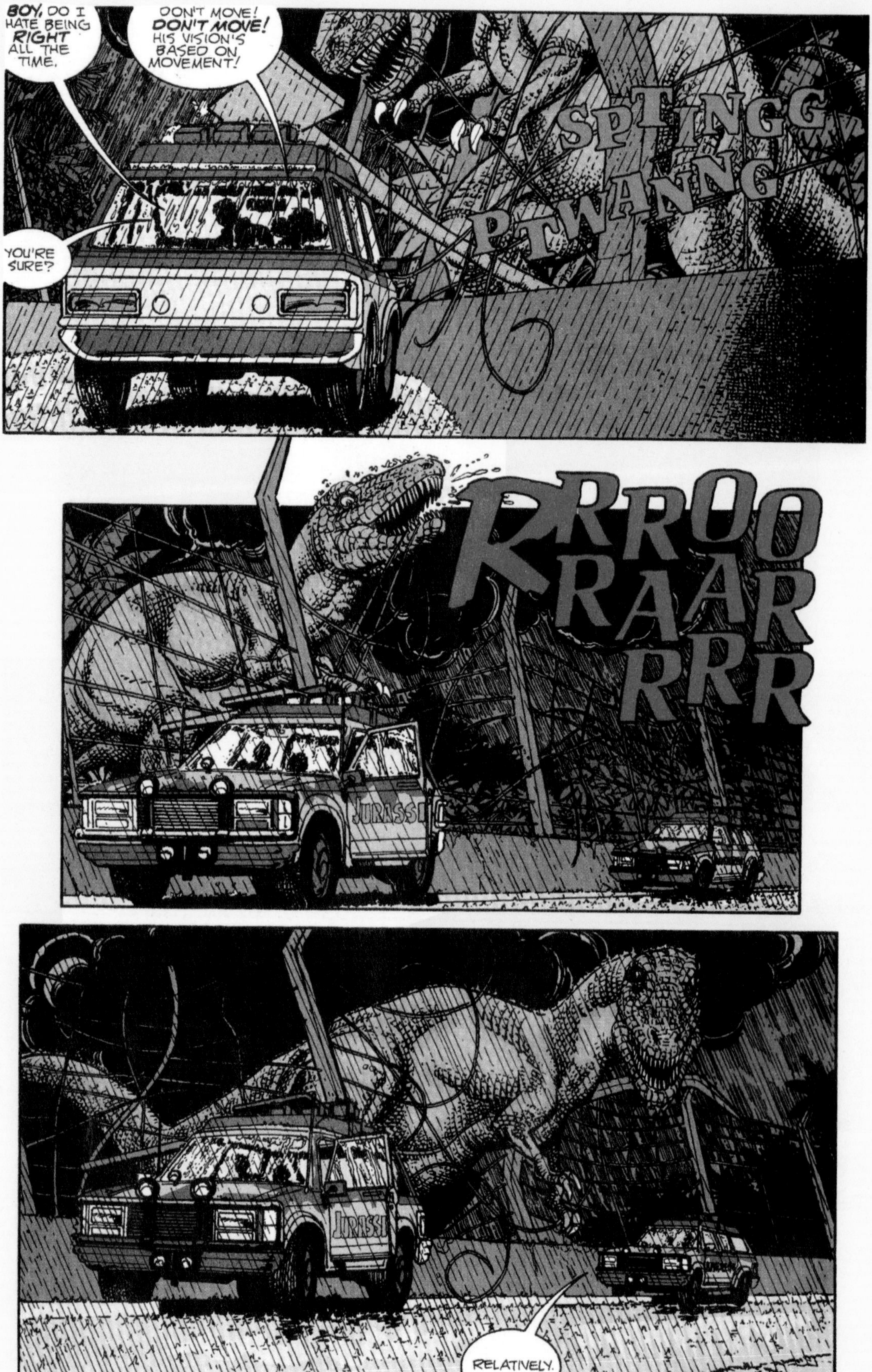
BOY, DO I HATE BEING RIGHT ALL THE TIME.
DON'T MOVE! DON'T MOVE! HIS VISION'S BASED ON MOVEMENT!
YOU'RE SURE?
SPTINGG
PTWANNG
RRROO RAAR RRR
JURASSI
RELATIVELY.

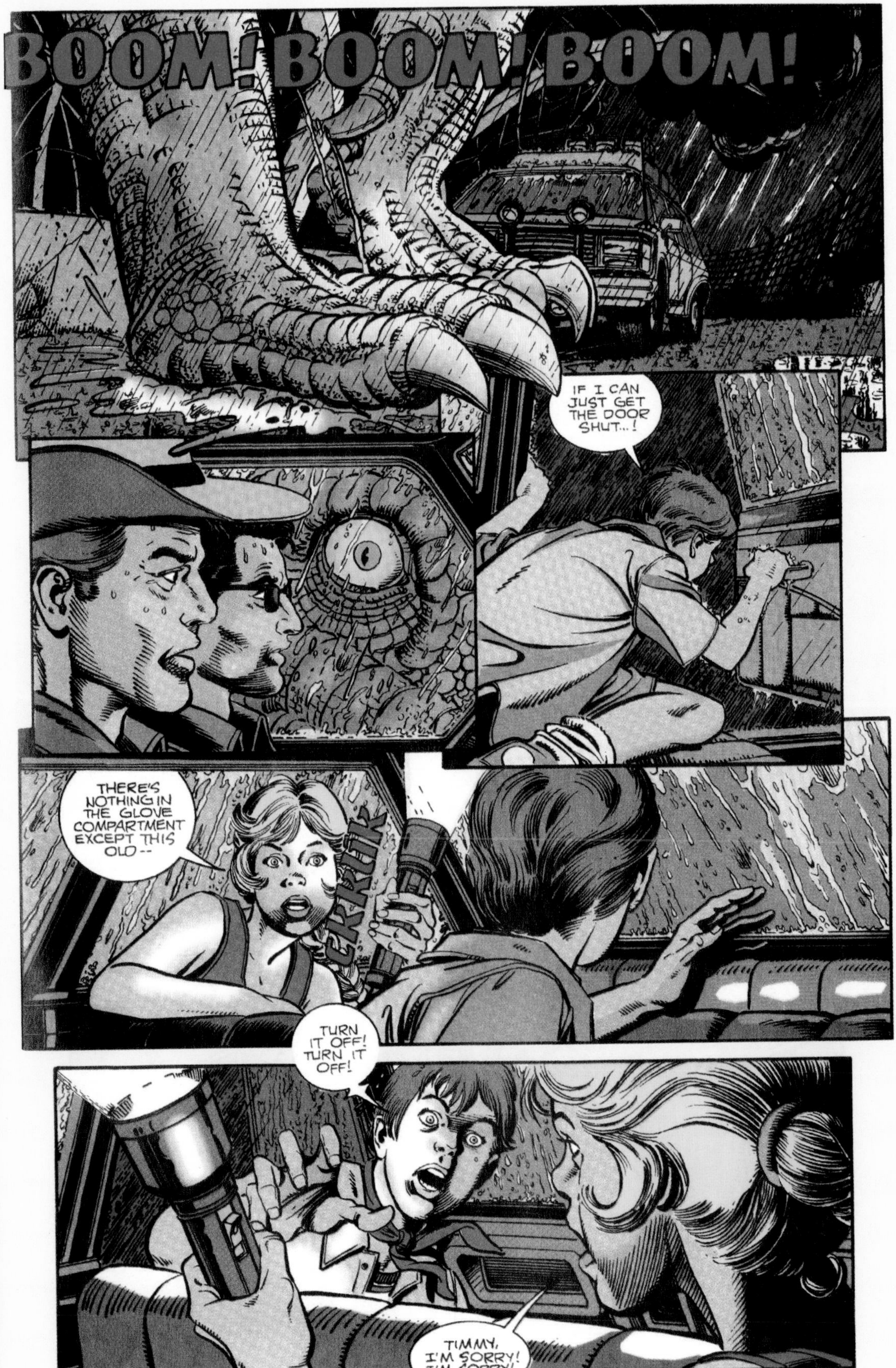
BOOM! BOOM! BOOM!
IF I CAN JUST GET THE DOOR SHUT...!
THERE'S NOTHING IN THE GLOVE COMPARTMENT EXCEPT THIS OLD --
CRKUK
TURN IT OFF! TURN IT OFF!
TIMMY, I'M SORRY! I'M SORRY!

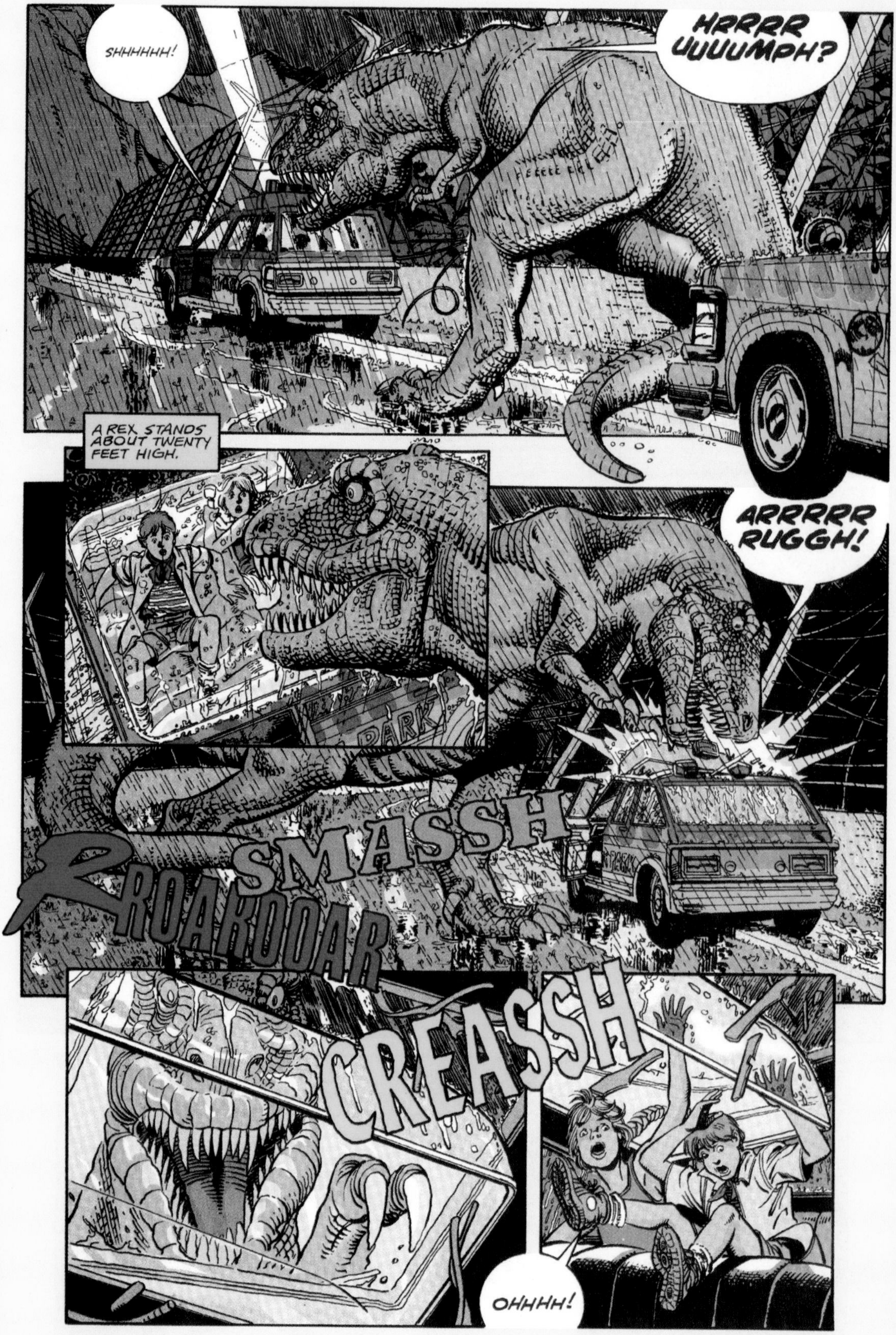
SHHHHHH!
HRRRR UUUUMPH?
A REX STANDS ABOUT TWENTY FEET HIGH.
PARK
ARRRRR RUGGH!
SMASSH
RROARRDAR
CREASSH
OHHHH!

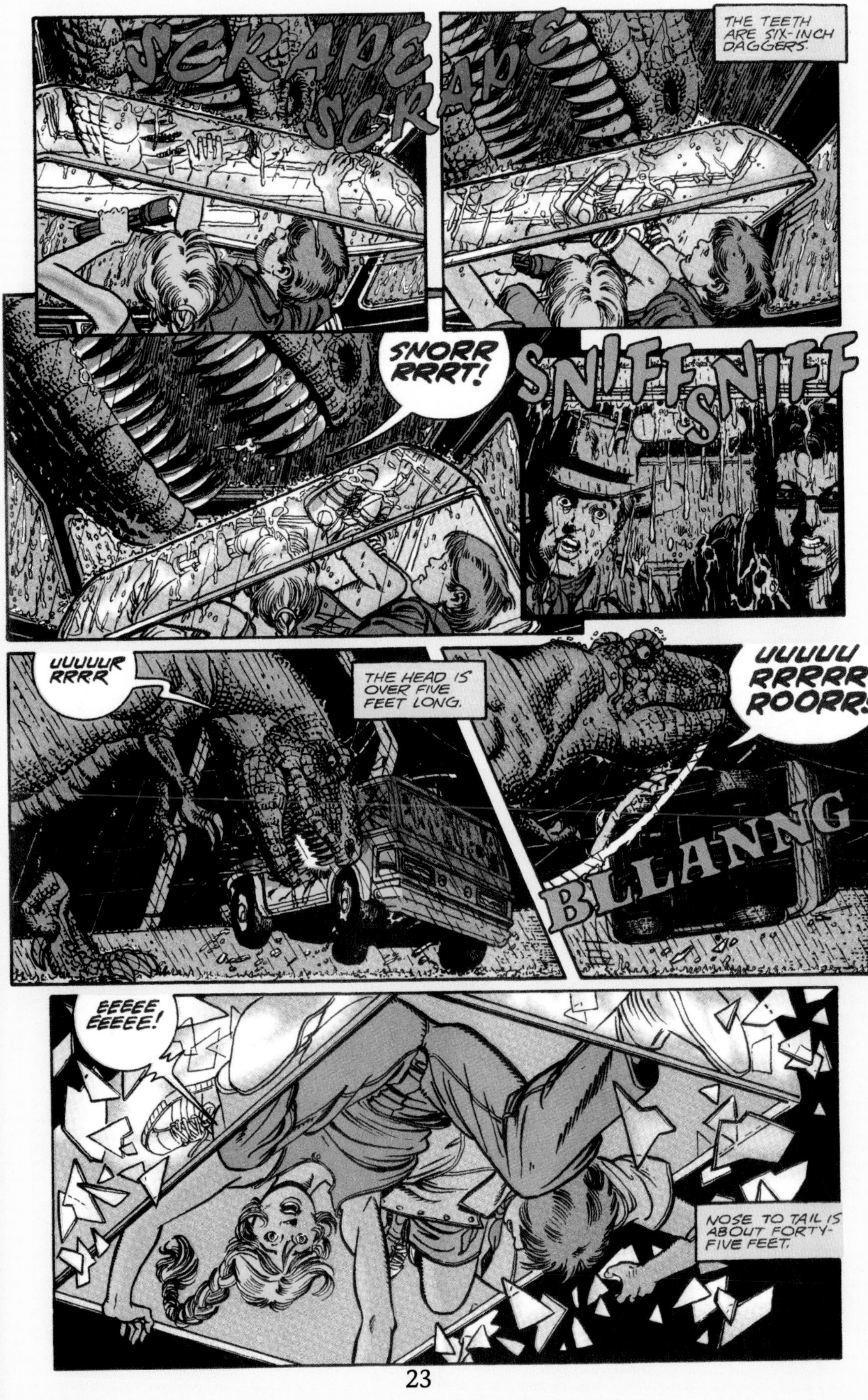
SCRAPE
SCRAPE
SCRAPE
THE TEETH ARE SIX-INCH DAGGERS.
SNORR RRRT!
SNIFF SNIFF
S
UUUUUR RRRR
THE HEAD IS OVER FIVE FEET LONG.
UUUUU RRRRR ROORR!
BLLANNG
EEEEE EEEEE!
NOSE TO TAIL IS ABOUT FORTY-FIVE FEET.

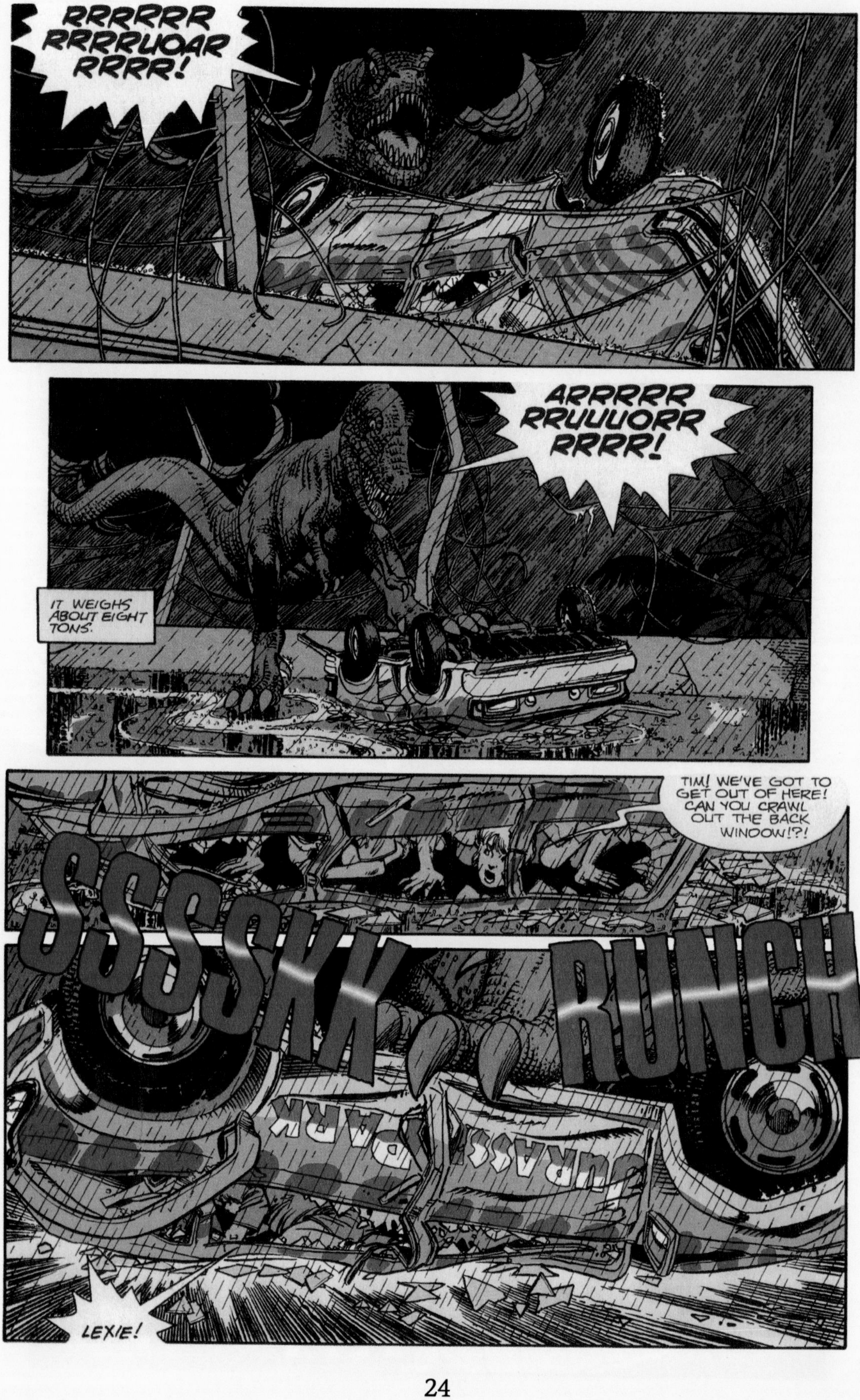
RRRRRR RRRRUOAR RRRR!
ARRRRR RRUUUORR RRRR!
IT WEIGHS ABOUT EIGHT TONS.
TIM! WE'VE GOT TO GET OUT OF HERE! CAN YOU CRAWL OUT THE BACK WINDOW!?!
SSSSKK
RUNCH
LEXIE!

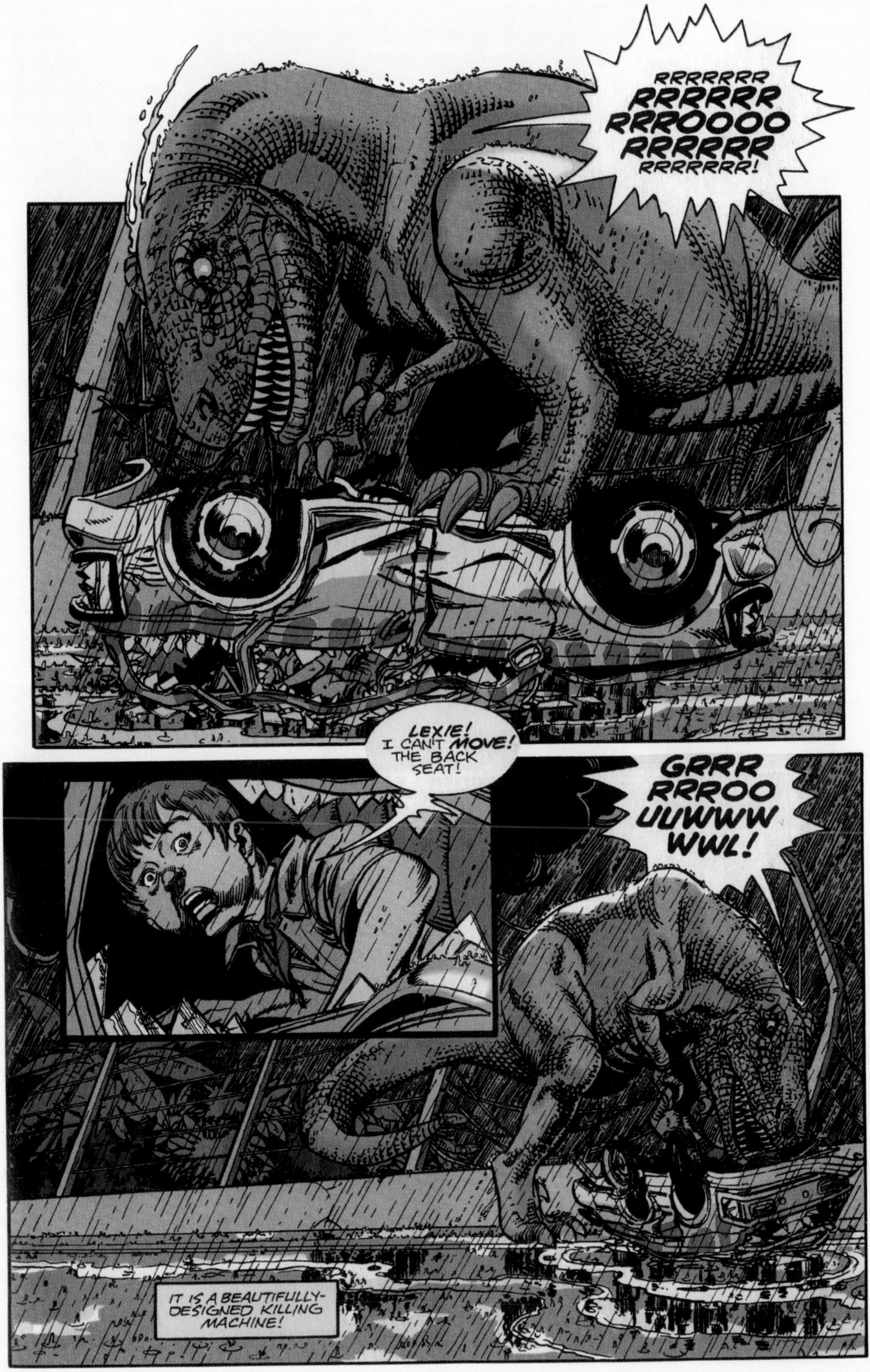
RRRRRRR RRRRRR RRROOOO RRRRRR RRRRRRR!
LEXIE! I CAN'T MOVE! THE BACK SEAT!
GRRR RRROO UUWWW WWL!
IT IS A BEAUTIFULLY-DESIGNED KILLING MACHINE!

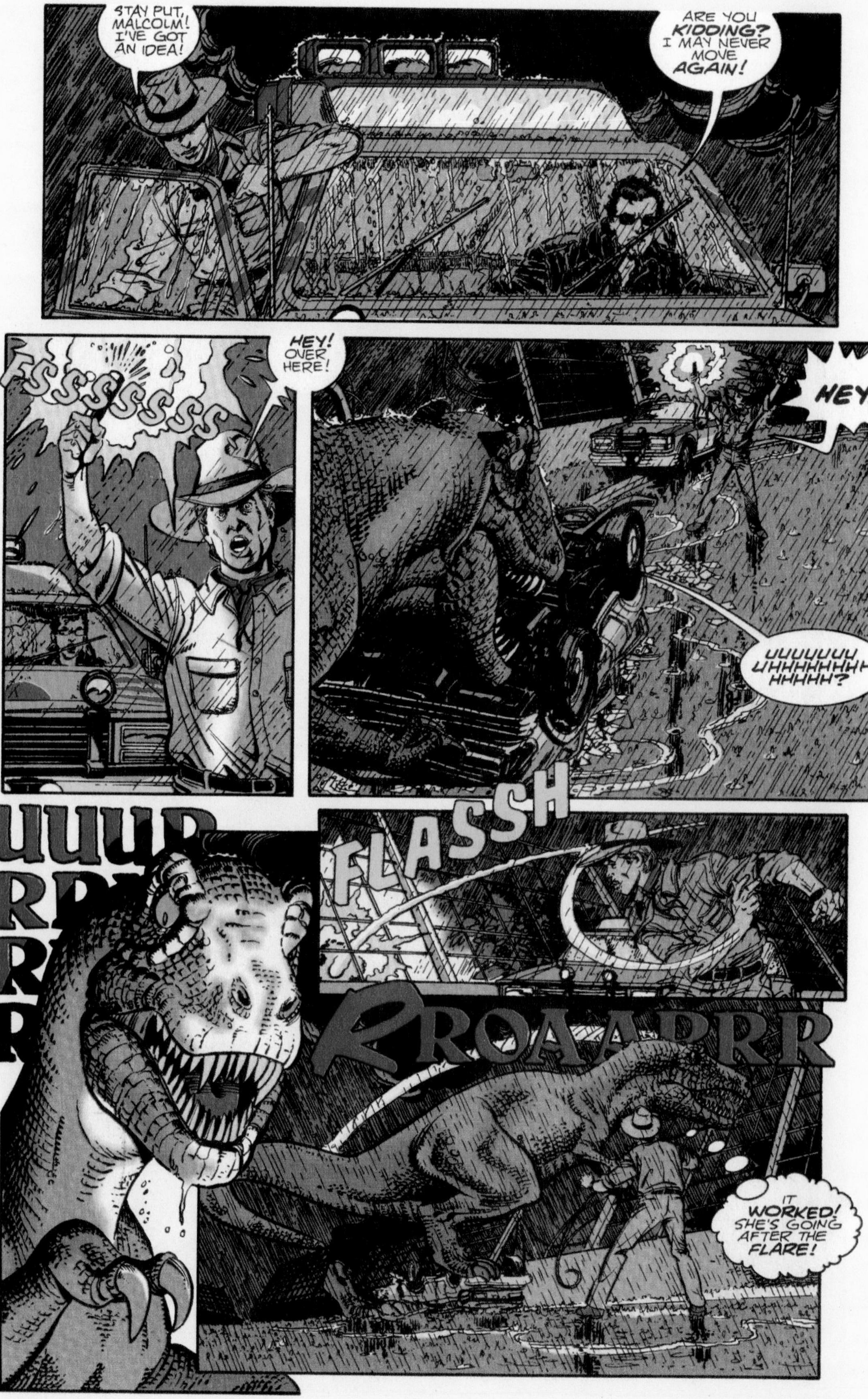

STAY PUT, MALCOLM! I'VE GOT AN IDEA!
ARE YOU KIDDING? I MAY NEVER MOVE AGAIN!
FSSSSSSS
HEY! OVER HERE!
HEY!
UUUUUUU UHHHHHHHH HHHHH?
UUUR RR R R
FLASSH
RROAARRR
IT WORKED! SHE'S GOING AFTER THE FLARE!

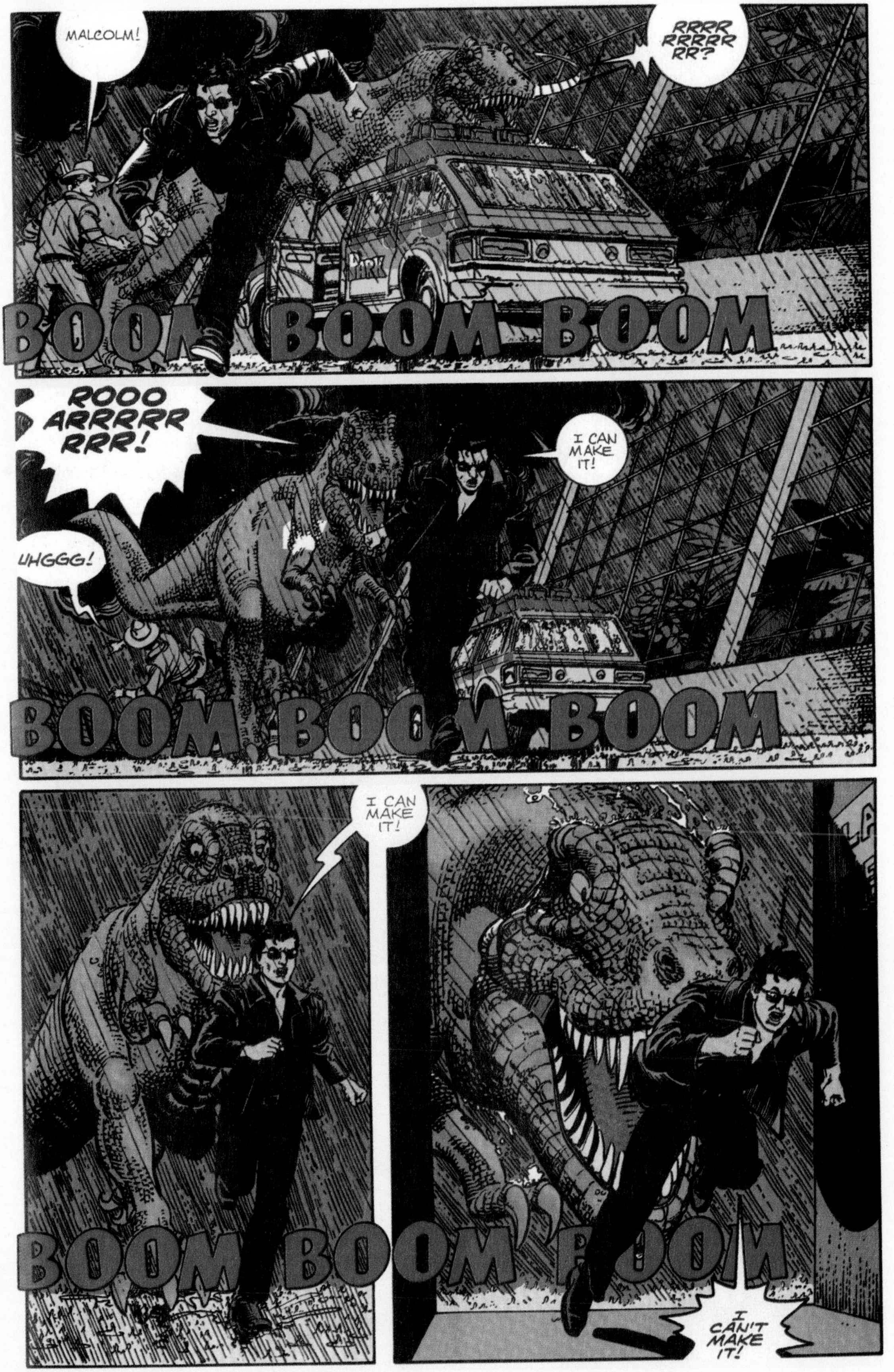
MALCOLM!
RRRR RRRRR RR?
BOOM BOOM BOOM
ROOO ARRRRR RRR!
I CAN MAKE IT!
UHGGG!
BOOM BOOM BOOM
I CAN MAKE IT!
BOOM BOOM BOOM
I CAN'T MAKE IT!

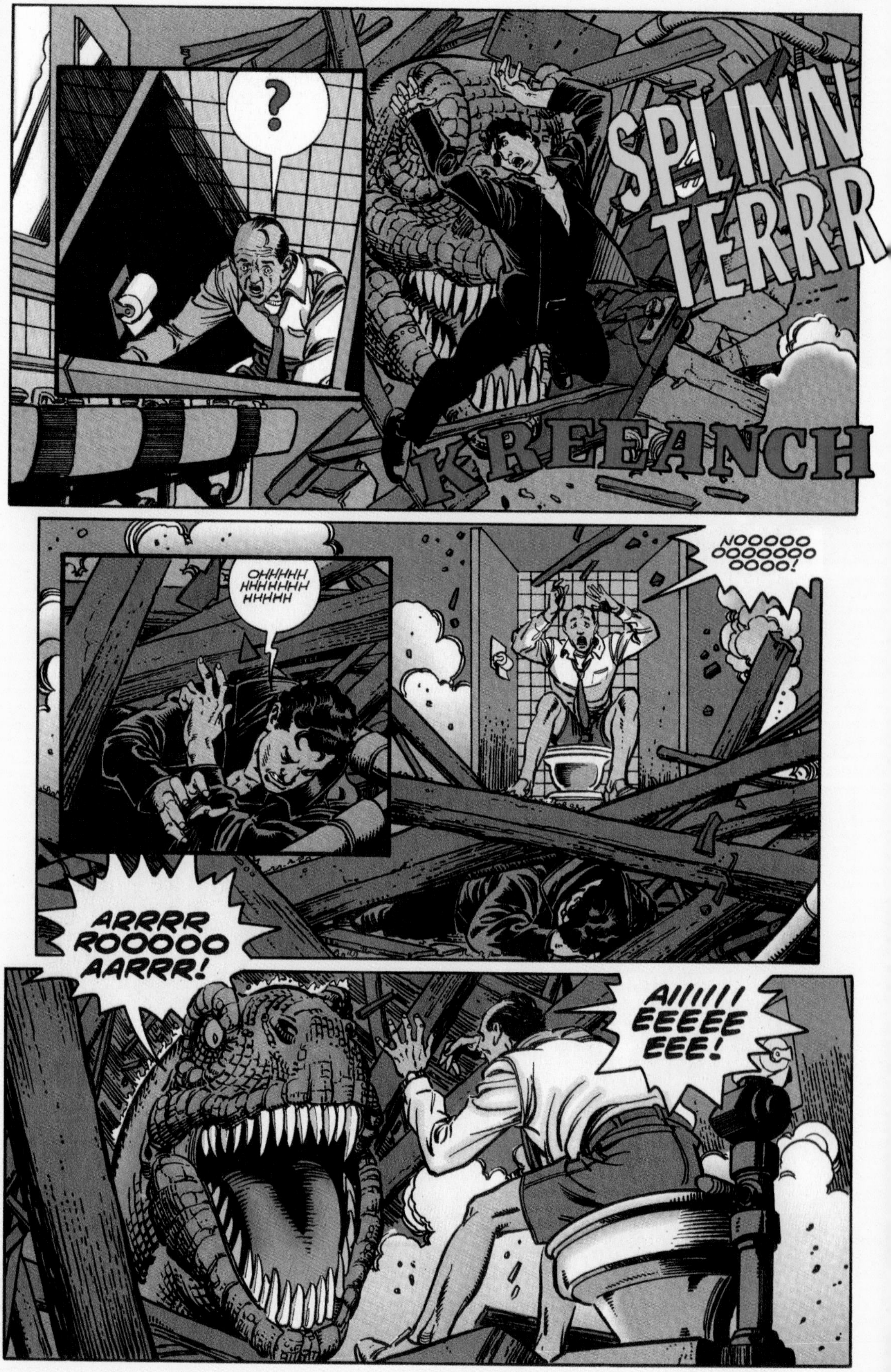
?
SPLINN
TERRR
KREEANCH
OHHHHH HHHHHHH HHHHH
NOOOOO OOOOOOO OOOO!
ARRRR ROOOOO AARRR!
AIIIIII EEEEE EEE!

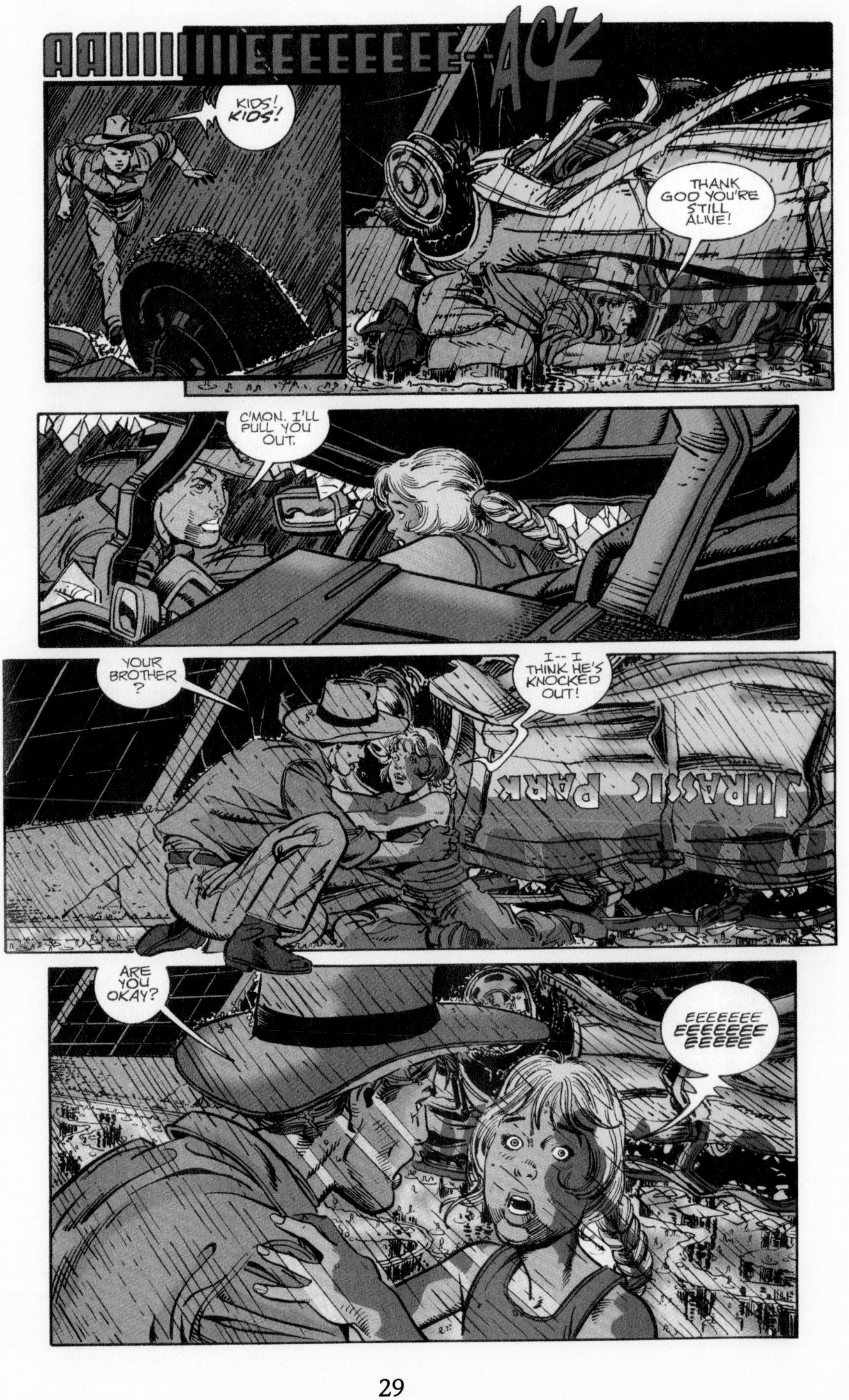
AAIIIIIIIIEEEEEEEEE--ACK
KIDS! KIDS!
THANK GOD YOU'RE STILL ALIVE!
C'MON. I'LL PULL YOU OUT.
YOUR BROTHER?
I-- I THINK HE'S KNOCKED OUT!
JURASSIC PARK
ARE YOU OKAY?
EEEEEEE EEEEEEE EEEEE

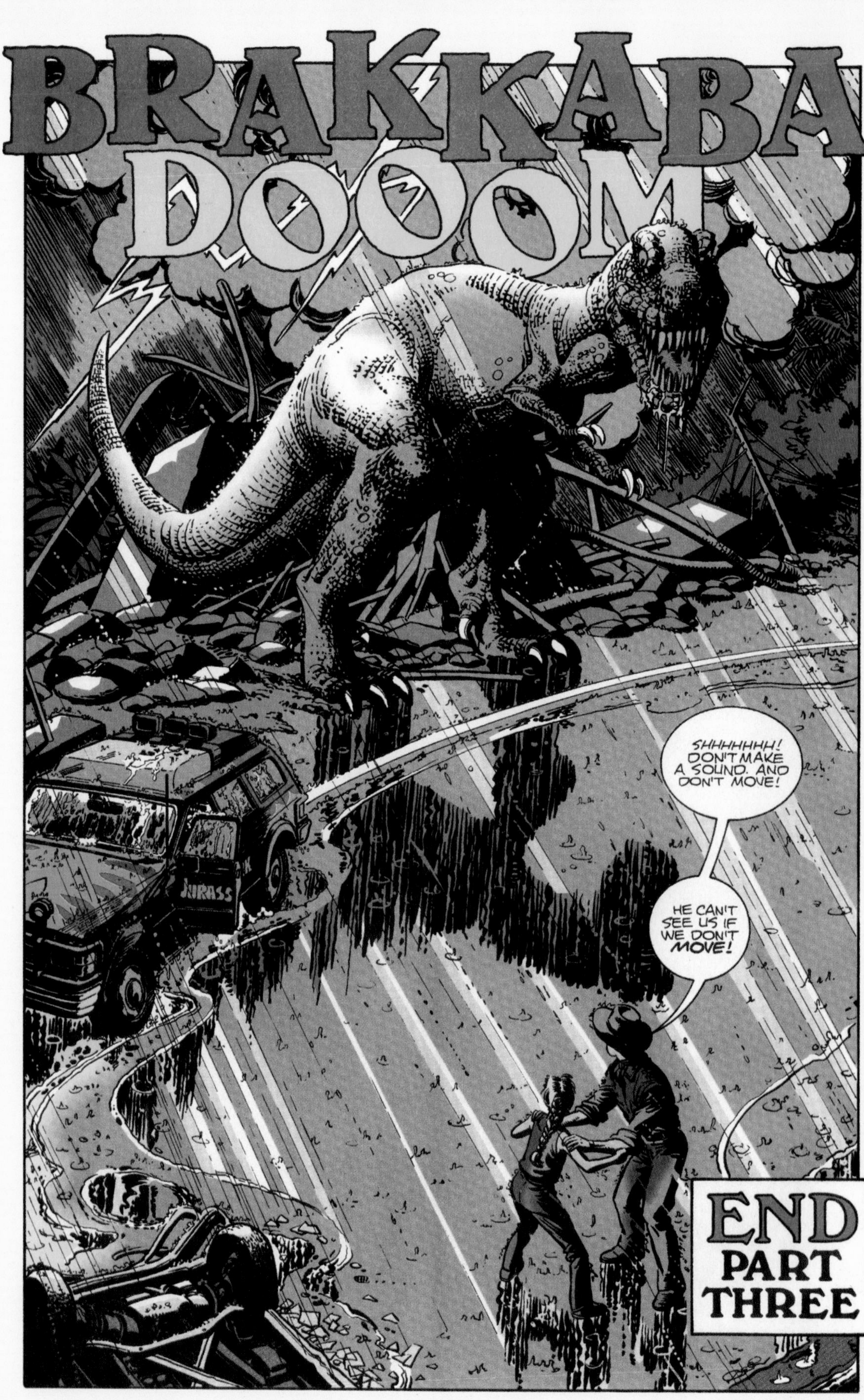
BRAKKABA DOOOM
SHHHHHHH! DON'T MAKE A SOUND. AND DON'T MOVE!
HE CAN'T SEE US IF WE DON'T MOVE!
END PART THREE